Numerius Meridius Pulcher

And

The Case of the Not So Virgin Vestal

(AUC 815)

With thanks to the Women in my Life BR and CR.

My love to you both for believing it possible

THE FAMILY

Numerius Meridius Pulcher --- A retired Capri boy and pleasure house owner, once notorious, now a not quite respectable citizen of Pompeii and Rome.

Metella--- The sister of Numerius, a proper Roman matron.

Burrus--- Retired Army husband of Metella and thorn in the side of Numerius.

Quintus--- Their son, Numerius' nephew. A bright young man without much direction.

Lucia---Their daughter approaching marriageable age.

OUTSIDE THE FAMILY

Pausina--- Once a famous beauty; now Chief Vestal.

*****Laelia**---The not so virgin Vestal.

Hesperia--- A friend and past employee of Numerius. Current owner of the Golden Wing, an infamous brothel for the wealthy of Rome.

Marcus Flavius--- Young scion of an old family, brother of Laelia. A young man
headed down a rocky path.

Old Flavius --- Respectable pillar of Roman Society. Father of Laelia and Marcus.

Quintus Aronius--- Another young man with too much given him for far too little.

Old Aronius--- A wealthy man trying to lead the good life.

*****Tigellinus**--- Prefecture of the Praetorian Guards.

THE SLAVES

Aristo--- The slave of Numerius and his long time companion.

Apollo--- A new gardener in the house of Burrus

Andronicus--- An ancient and favored slave belonging to Numerius, who serves as doorkeeper and head gardener in the house of Burrus.

Chloe---The personal slave of Laelia and hard to find.

Phillipia---An old flame of Aristo's.

* Historical character

Prologue

In the spring of AUC 815 my Pompeii house was undergoing major renovation to repair the earthquake damage it had received in February of that year, and so I traveled to Rome to occupy a new home I was having built on the Quirinal Hill. I had been promised it would be ready for my arrival, but like so many promises made in Rome, it came to nothing. Rome may well be the center of the world, but in many ways that only means that it is the center of a giant cesspool. All roads lead to Rome, the saying goes. Unfortunately, the people who take those roads into our capitol find them clogged with conmen, common thieves, liars, cheats, charlatans and murderers. In that eighth year of the rule of Nero not all of them came from out of town.

As I entered Rome that early morning prepared to move into my new house, a young girl was also preparing for a new life. Like me she was being moved along on a wave of anticipation. Like me she would be

disappointed. Within the day, unlike me, she would be dead. I came to call it The Case of the Not So Virgin Vestal.

Chapter 1

We were in Rome and the new house was not ready.
For a moment, in my irritation, I simply wanted to climb back into
the litter and give the order to my boys to head straight back to
Pompeii.   Rome is frustrating, and nothing there is ever
accomplished on time. The greatest city in the world, indeed. We
couldn't make the trip home by evening, but we could spend the
night on the way. There were friends we could seek hospitality from
or, less attractively, inns along the way, but the fact was that the
Pompeii house was still under repairs as a result of the recent
earthquake. Heading home was not an option. For the moment I
was, for all intent and purposes, homeless.

I stood looking at the unhinged doors and stacks of tiles meant for the mosaic floor of the entry. There was much left undone although I had been assured that all would be ready for our arrival. So much for the word of architects, contractors and artisans. Money can buy you innumerable things in Rome but attention to deadlines is evidently not one of them.

I glanced for input over to Aristo who stood waiting for the storm to pass. He wisely gave none. There were options. We could camp out in the gardens. We could look for lodgings. It wouldn't be easy at this time of day to acquire rooms for me, Aristo, the litter bearers, a cook and his family that I'd brought from Pompeii, the four carts and their accompanying drivers and oxen, and the few house slaves that I had decided would take charge of the Rome house. All told we were well over twenty men, women and beasts, closer to thirty was my guess. Aristo would have known to the child. I looked again at Aristo.

"Well..." it was an admission of defeat, an indication that I was ready to listen to reason. It was all he needed.

"The carts and drivers will have to remain here. They will be banned from the streets before they could get anywhere. The stables and out buildings will hold the majority of the others and I can find suitable lodgings for the cook and his family. He won't suffer gladly staying in make-do circumstances, and you want to keep him happy.

As for you, me and the litter bearers, well, we could look for rooms, but that will be difficult on such short notice or..." his voice trailed off, knowing I would not welcome the final suggestion.

It was, of course, the only sensible solution, but I dreaded it. The one place I did not want to be was stuck for an unknown span of time with Burrus. No, having to accept the hospitality of my sister Metella and her husband Burrus was not something I looked forward to. The history was long, and it didn't matter that they lived in a house that was technically mine. To spend the next two or three weeks under the same roof with my brother-in-law was not appealing. The man was insufferable, had always been so. Not unattractive of course; I could see why my sister had accepted the Burrus offer. Twenty years later the man was still attractive in a bullish sort of way, an aging Marc Antony, dashing but a bit spoiled and softened by his love of wine and the good life. Burrus was not the man I would have chosen for my sister, but all that had happened before I found and reclaimed her.

Burrus, unlike my sister Metella, I had already been all too well acquainted with. It had not been a pleasant surprise that within the hour of finally finding my sister I had also found her to be married to Quintus Lucius Burrus. I consoled myself with the thought that all of that was in the past and mattered little. So, despite the past between us I had decided that, for my sister's sake, I would make peace with Burrus. Eventually that led to allowing them to move into my house on the Palatine. Once there they had rapidly produced my nephew, Quintus, and a niece, Lucia, both delightful children when out from under the direct influence of their father. Besides, Metella seemed happy and that was worth putting up with Quintus Lucius Burrus, at least when it couldn't be avoided. The prospect of the next two or three weeks under the same roof was daunting, but I supposed it had to be done.

"We're going to the Palatine," I said to Aristo, my head slave and constant companion. "Tell the others to stay here and wait for the rest of the furniture. They'll have to pull the wagons into the garden. Tell Doribus to keep them well guarded. This is Rome, not Pompeii. I'll go ahead. You come tonight after they let the carts in. I'll try not to kill Burrus before you get there." I know how to sound as if I'm in charge. Aristo would see to it all.

Aristo smiled. "Absence has failed to make the heart grow fonder?"

"One of these days you'll find yourself for sale."

"Good, then I'll start saving up my money." He smiled again, this time for real. "But, you're not getting rid of me that easily."

"You had best save up a good deal of it." I answered with a smile I knew would reach him. I would have preferred to reach out and touch the strong arm for just a second, but the slave would have been appalled at such public display. Aristo has a very strict sense of what is appropriate. Physical contact of an affectionate variety in public between a slave and a master would be considered unseemly. In truth Aristo was a slave in name only. He had long since been offered his freedom and refused. "When you die, then I will be free," Aristo had said, "but not until then."

"Later then," I said, turning to the litter. "Let's get up to the Palatine House, boys." I climbed in and lay back on an array of new silk upholstered cushions and prepared to reacquaint myself with the familiar sights of Rome. Aristo signaling the litter bearers, grinned, and waved us off.

Rome had changed since my last visit. A surge of construction added to the cacophony of the city's streets; everywhere new buildings were sprouting up and up, higher and higher. Times were good for Rome, at least so it seemed at that point in time. New construction, renovation of the old, public works, everything pointed to the prosperity and well being of the Empire.

I considered a detour to the Golden Wing in order to visit my old friend Hesperia, but both she and Aristo would be disappointed if the slave were not included in my visit. Besides they would be in the midst of preparations for a night's work there. Aristo was a favorite of Hesperia and had been since he arrived at The Golden Wing as a young boy, no older than twelve or so.   I had already put her in charge of the staff by then, although I still oversaw the finer details on a daily basis. She had been the first to recognize Aristo's special qualities.

No, I couldn't have made a first visit to Hesperia after so long without being accompanied by Aristo; so I decided it wiser to keep on course, working our way through the forum and heading up the hill to the old house on the Palatine. As we juggled the throng of foot traffic past the House of Vestals, I thought I saw Pausina, or someone who might have been Pausina, just a glimpse, standing alone in the garden looking out. She had done well for herself. The position of Chief Vestal is an important one and carries a good deal of power. When I had known her she had not been so powerful, neither of us had. She was another part of my past that unremittingly lifted its ugly head when in Rome.   It was unavoidable; simply part and parcel of being in Rome. I constantly run into the past. It haunts me here whereas in Pompeii there were rumors of course, but for the most part just that, not many there were aware of the hard reality of the facts. Here I ran into that reality almost daily. Ten years is long enough for fact to come mixed with legend, but not quite long enough for forgetfulness in the scandal hungry social circles of Rome. I still run into the men who had frequented the Golden Wing, and the stories and whispers of the past still follow me whenever I am in

Rome. That, no doubt, contributes to some of my discomfort with Burrus. Quintus Lucius Burrus was an all too real part of that past, an unsavory part as far as I was concerned. Maybe it was hard for Burrus as well. The tables have turned and we both have to live with it. As far as I knew, my sister knew nothing about it and that was the way I wished for it to stay. There was nothing to be gained by her knowing our previous connection. There had been little to it anyway. It had all taken place in the distant past, another world as far as I was concerned.

The old house of the Meridii, the house that I had inherited when adopted by Numerius Meridius and took up his name with the added cognomen Pulcher, was situated on the Palatine. It was one of the old style homes, near the sprawling new palaces and complexes of hidden bureaucracy that Augustus and Livia had built. Its severity from the street belied the tasteful calmness once inside the heavy barred doors. It was one of the oldest houses on the hill, the Numerius Meridius family having built it back in the old days of the Republic. That it had come to me with Old Numerius' adoption and will had certainly scandalized the neighbors. They still kept their distance and that had suited me for the short time I had lived in the house before moving in my sister, Metella and her husband. It had been harder on them. My brother-in-law, Burrus, might only be a narrow striper, but it could still be socially awkward being a relative of Numerius Meridius Pulcher, formerly known as Hylas. I had to give the man that. Some husbands would have divorced Metella when they had discovered the connection, and whether it was because of love or the money involved mattered little when it came to facing the public perceptions of the multiple ladders of social machinery of Rome. Secretly however, I suspected that even if he had remained out of love, and I believed he did love her, the ready money made it all the easier for Burrus to bear.

The litter turned the final corner and began the climb to the end of the street where the house lay. I shifted inside the luxurious interior. The street always made me uncomfortable, whether it was the nearness of my brother-in-law, the disdain of the neighbors or both, I was never quite sure. The litter was overly ostentatious for this neighborhood. I should have had them drop me off at the turn and finished the trip on foot, except that too would have subjected me to stares. At the new house the litter would be just one of the numerous ostentations of that overdone neighborhood. Here in this reserved neighborhood, it stuck out like a whore sharing a table and jug with a Vestal outside the corner wine shop. Well, such was life, and old Numerius would have gotten a good amount of pleasure out of setting the tongues of neighbors a-twittering. The old man had been kind to me. When one has led an early life such as mine, one rarely forgets a kindness. Old Numerius had been very kind and provided me with a life that was most comfortable. I have always needed to honor his memory. So, I smiled and gathered myself for a grand exit as the men put the litter down in front of the door. Let them stare.

A wizened old man opened the door in response to my knock. "Hallo, Numerius Meridius Pulcher," the doorman beamed toothlessly. "We didn't know you were coming, but the Mistress will be delighted. Come in, come in."

"Good to see you Andronicus," I said grasping the old man's shoulders. "I've brought you something new from the Pompeii garden. Aristo will be bringing it with him later. I think you will like it. If anyone can make it grow here in Rome, you can." The old slave did wonders with the cramped garden of the Palatine house and I was constantly bringing something new for him to fuss over.

"You spoil me," the old man grinned. "I hope I can find a place for it. You have brought me so much."

"Oh, I've no doubt you'll find a place. Well, lock us back in and run tell Metella that I'm here and will be staying for a while."

"She will be delighted. How long should I tell her? She'll want to know."

"Oh, just long enough to make sure her husband is thoroughly disgusted."

The old slave rolled his eyes and laughed. "That's not such a long time. Go ahead and look over what I've done in the garden. The rose trees you brought last time are in bloom. I'll have the Mistress join you. She'll be pleased. But...," the old man grinned wickedly, "...unfortunately, the Master is out."

"In that case have some of his best wine sent out. Maybe he has some of the Falernian left that I sent him last time. In any case I've brought him a few amphorae of a Caecuban which is delightful and becoming hard to find. I could use something to wash down this dust of Rome." I watched the old man exit and made my own way to the garden at the back of the house. Andronicus had indeed succeeded expectations. The garden was blooming with carefully tended roses and oleander, ivy, lilies, larkspur, feverfew and periwinkle. It could have been a paradise far, far from urban realities of Rome. The old man, Andronicus, knew his gardening. I would have loved to set him free in my garden at the Pompeii house, but the old slave had been born and bred in this house and to take him from it at such an advanced age would be unthinkable. Maybe I needed to send one of the Pompeii gardeners up to Rome in order to pick the old man's brain, and I certainly could see to his having a good deal of input on the garden of new house on the Quirinal Hill.

As I was running the plan through my mind, the foliage at one end of the garden parted expelling the half stripped bulk of an Adonis. I was surprised, perhaps more by the beauty of the man than his sudden appearance from the greenery. He bore an incredible likeness to a Greek statue I had bought for my house in Pompeii; unfortunately, it had been broken to pieces during the recent earthquake. This man who stared so calmly at me could have been the model for it. I blinked wondering if he would disappear or at least reappear in a more realistic form.

"And who might you be?" I asked, caught off guard. "I am Numerius, the brother of the Mistress. In my youth and then in the long years of business at the Golden Wing I had long since become a connoisseur of beauty, both feminine and masculine. I was, as a rule, unmoved by it after all the years spent with beauties that somehow never failed to go deeper than their surfaces, but this young man was indeed extraordinary, that much was obvious at first glance.

"You must be new," I said a little unnerved at my being so flustered by a slave in the garden of a house I owned. I waited for the Adonis to answer, but the young man merely blinked at me. "You do belong here don't you?" Again I waited. The Adonis neither spoke nor moved. I would have thought him an apparition except that I could see the expanding chest as he breathed.

"And your name?" I tried again this time in Greek, as often as not that seemed to be the commonly known language of many slaves new to Rome.

"He won't answer you, my dear," said Metella coming through the atrium into the garden. "He seems quite mute, or at least to speak some language we've yet to discover. He's Andronicus' new trainee. He picked this one out himself. And at a very pretty price I might add. But Andronicus was set on him."

"What's the old devil up to? The lad looks more like a fancy house stud than a gardener." I turned, laughed and embraced Metella, lifting her from the floor.

"I know, I know. Burrus used even harsher terms when he first saw him, but Andronicus assures us the boy is a gardener, and so it seems he is. Now put me down." I did.

"I'm surprised Burrus allows him in the house."

"Don't be ridiculous. He's a gardener."

"A gardener?"

"Well, just look at the place. He practically lives out here rain or shine and Andronicus, as you know, spends as much time out here as possible. The two seem to get along winningly and you know how hard to please Andronicus can be."

"Why that sly dirty old…"

"Now Numerius, don't. Not everyone has the same devious mind you have. Don't pick on old Andronicus. He adores you."

"Ah, all the more proof. We all know where I came from."

"Now don't. Do be serious." She smiled, turned to the slave and motioned with her hand toward the area the man had come from. "You can go back to work, Apollo."

I laughed. "You're kidding?

"No, that was his name when he got here. It was written on a little tablet hung around his neck."

"Oh well, thanks be to the gods! They do occasionally fulfill our hopes."

Metella tried not to smile. "Sit down, Numerius. Leave my gardener alone and talk to me. You're supposed to be here to see me after all."

"Actually I had no choice, the house in Pompeii has been taken over by the repairmen and the new house here isn't ready yet. I'm afraid you'll have to put up with me for a while, until one of the two becomes habitable again."

"We love your visits, and they don't come often enough."

"We? Who exactly are you including in that 'We'."

"Don't start, you big fool. The children and I love to see you and you know it very well."

"And Burrus?"

"Burrus is always pleased to see you."

"What a wonderful liar you are, lady. From the look on your face I would almost believe it." I winked at her. It was true. I would have been far less successful in life if all people could lie as well as my sister. Perhaps it is because she wanted to believe it so much. Metella's lies simply made the world a better place to live in. Maybe it was a gift, and with the early life she had been through the gods knew she deserved whatever happiness she had found.

Andronicus himself brought the salver with the wine and bits of cheese and dried fruits into the garden. I accepted the wine from the old man. "It's beautiful," I said waving my hand at the surroundings. "You are a miracle worker. Those rose trees I brought you the last time we were here are out-blooming the ones we have in Pompeii. Whatever have you done to them? Corvinus says they're very tricky bloomers."

"They like a careful hand." The old man said putting down the tray.

"So you won't tell me your secrets? Well, never mind. They are splendid, old man, splendid indeed."

Andronicus grinned broadly, nodded and walked back to the house without a word, his back straighter and head higher than his years had right to expect.

"So tell me about the children, young Quintus and Lucia?" I turned back to Metella. "How are they doing? Lucia must be springing up by now. Are you turning her into the respectable ideal of a young Roman lady, readying her for some spectacular match? Got any young man in mind?"

"It's a bit early for that, Numerius," Metella smiled and waved her hand at the thought. "I'm not ready to give her up quite yet. But yes, we are pleased. She is a joy as she has always been."

"And the boy? How is Quintus?"

Metella shifted slightly in her chair and sighed. "Constantly out with his friends. Too much drinking and carousing I suspect, but Burrus merely laughs and tells me that it's a stage all young men go through. I would like to see him be more serious about his future."

"For once I agree with Burrus, but don't tell him I said so. He's right though. Let the boy have some fun, Metella. Life will change him soon enough. Nothing serious is there?"

"Serious, no...just a lack of direction."

"Give him time, Metella," I said patting her hand. "You'll have no worries with that one. I can assure you of that. Unless of course he grows up like his father," I added with a grin, always ready to take a swipe at the man.

"Don't start, Numerius. Burrus is a fine man. He makes me happy."

"How is the old bull?"

"Quite well, actually. You know Burrus, nothing seems to phase him."

"Indeed I do. Nothing will stop that man," I said with a harder edge than I had meant.

Metella stopped, her eyes blinking coldly for just a moment before continuing. "Enough, Numerius. I don't know why the two of you insist on pretending that you dislike each other so intently. It can fray upon one's nerves."

"Force of habit," I said with a smile. "But enough of that, I promise to be nice."

"Good. Now tell me about Pompeii. We've heard bits and pieces of course, but not from anyone who was actually there. Was the damage extensive? Is the house reparable or will you have to rebuild?"

"Messy but not disastrous," and I launched into my stock story on the shaking of Pompeii and the surrounding areas that had taken place a few months prior.

I sat on for a while after Metella had excused herself to check on dinner preparations. I thought to enjoy the garden but found myself casually keeping an eye on the slave Apollo's progress around the garden as he dug, planted and trimmed, a work of beauty in himself and seemingly oblivious to all but his task. Had there been scars he would have passed as a gladiator. It was a study in contrasts to watch the muscle bound Apollo (for an Apollo or young Jupiter he was indeed) work so gently and deftly with the delicate flowers and lush foliage.

I sat idle, mesmerized in my watching until Aristo arrived with my things. Then I was encouraged to go off to ready myself for dinner, but not before Aristo and Apollo caught sight of each other and flexed their muscles at one another in instant dislike. It was amusing to me, but I took Aristo off to my rooms before things had a chance to escalate.

"A gardener, indeed," Aristo muttered in Greek, setting out my various jars of ointments, paint, and kohl. It was a habit he had when irritated, switching from Latin to his native tongue and muttering to himself as if I weren't there, all the while knowing full well I understood everything he said. "Looks like something you would have bought for the Golden Wing."

I smiled. "Now that would have been a money maker, don't you think?"

Aristo clicked his tongue and pulled the comb roughly through my hair and changed back to Latin. "No doubt, if one goes for that Greek marble statue look. Probably not one brain in that whole hulk of a body."

"A brain is not always absolutely necessary for such purposes," I grinned wincing at the dig of the comb but unable to resist egging him on. "Actually a brain is low on the list of requisites."

"A one nighter," he muttered again in Greek, with the derogative term used in the business for especially attractive persons who, for whatever reasons, failed to entice more than once per customer. "Quiet now, I need to touch up the eyes. They're showing your lack of sleep," he said picking up a fine brush and putting an end to any more conversation.

Chapter 2

I was late for dinner. I am rather consistently rather late; the careful artifice of my appearance is not easily or quickly accomplished and I am not unknowing about the effects of a staged entrance, how once the others were seated, conversation would momentarily stand still and all eyes follow the seating of the late comer. It's vanity no doubt, but it has been a good part of my life and old habits die hard. I slipped onto the couch next to Lucia on Burrus' right and across from young Quintus, keenly aware of the wide eyed approval of my niece and nephew, while Metella deftly figured the amount and cost of the silk which changed colors under the light and had cost me a small fortune. I was glad I had brought more for her and Lucia. I enjoyed spoiling the two of them with such luxuries.

Even Burrus, for a moment, took it all in with a dropped jaw, before composing himself.

"I come bearing presents," I smiled offering my glass to the slave who stood ready to fill it with Burrus' wine. "More of this silk for the ladies, a blue/green for you Metella and a honeyed gold for our Lucia, here, with a lovely coral pendent and earrings that some devious merchant said I must have to go with the cloth. It's amazing stuff, the way the material acts under the light as you move."

"You shouldn't have, Numerius..." Metella began effusively.

"Oh, Uncle,..." started Lucia with just the look that made these extravagances worth my while.

I waved them away. "What else am I to do with my ill got gains if not spoil my family? And for Burrus his favorite garum as usual, and a few amphorae of some Caecuban that I know you will enjoy. "   Even he grinned his thanks.   Burrus loved the heavy fish sauce and used it liberally on his food. To me it was overrated, making everything taste the same and totally eclipsing the taste of the food, but Romans love it and insist on having it at table. The wine he would always welcome as well. The man could down a formidable amount of the stuff, always could.

"Best damn garum I've ever had. Whatever Aulus Umbricus Scaurus does to his sauce I wish the Roman makers would find it out. Thank you, Numerius. You know I'll enjoy it."

"Oh, yes, and for you, Quintus, I must have brought something for you, but at the moment it escapes me. Probably some book or other to help you with your studies. You are studying aren't you?"

The boy smiled back unconvinced by my foolery. "Not if I can escape it, Uncle. I study only when Mother absolutely beats me into submission. The study of Latin and Greek is more palatable when I've been beaten black and blue and senseless."

"Wicked boy!" I laughed and turned to Metella. "You really should beat him you know. Builds character."

My sister smiled and looked fondly at her eldest. "Oh, he's not quite that bad, brother. Still there are times..." She let her voice trail off in an adoring smile.

"Well, then maybe it wasn't a book after all. Maybe it was something you'll find in the stables at my new house. Maybe something with four legs."

"You brought me a horse?" Quintus nearly ejected himself from off the couch he was lying on. "I can't believe it."

"It could be a dog. They have four legs, as do cats, even mice and rats as I remember it. Four legs could be just about anything..."

"But it's a horse, isn't it?" demanded the boy totally sure of himself. "Tell me it's a horse, Numerius"

"Yes. Yes, I'm afraid you're right, but that's all I'm saying for the time being. You'll have to wait until you see him...her...it. Aristo will take you over in the morning. I think you'll be pleased."

"Now, that's what I call an extravagant gift," bellowed Burrus from across the table with a broad grin and wink directed at his son. "He should be pleased."

"I know I will be," the boy said throwing a peach across the table which I caught easily and threw back at him.

"There will be no throwing food," interjected Metella. "Enough of this, now. We've interrupted dinner long enough. Cook will be furious if we dawdle any longer and it gets cold." She nodded to one of the slaves standing ready at the door. "Tell them to bring in the next course, Anthia."

Dinner continued and I was able to look at this little family of mine. Lucia was indeed blossoming into a young woman. Quintus grew more attractive and manly by the visit. Even Burrus seemed as robust as ever, but my attention was drawn to Metella. Under the carefully applied cosmetics she looked seriously tired. I had missed it earlier. Here amongst the youth of her children and the unflagging good health of Burrus I was able to judge better. Fragility lay beneath the skin. Maybe it was just the passing of time, but I didn't feel comfortable with it and made up my mind to confront her about it later. It certainly wasn't the type of thing she would talk about at dinner, if I could get her to talk about it at all.

Burrus too seemed not quite himself tonight, but it had nothing to do with his appearance of health. Drinking as always, maybe the slightest bit more than usual, but he seemed a little preoccupied and tense, glancing over at Quintus every few minutes as if waiting for the boy to do something, whether to praise or defile I couldn't tell but it was clear he expected something of the boy and that he wasn't getting it. Several times I caught glances from Metella questioning him.

My brother-in-law shrugged at her as if to say 'whatever are you going on about?' Then he took a heavy gulp of his wine and cleared his throat. "Well, what do you think of our Young Quintus, Numerius?" he asked me over the top of his wine goblet. "Look at those shoulders, the muscle on the boy. Soon, he'll rival me at that age, don't you think?"

"He is a good looking lad which is to be expected with his parentage." I said it easily, for it was true. And the boy was becoming quite the looker – not the massive muscles of Burrus. He was built trimmer and with the grace of his mother. Burrus on the other hand had always had massive muscles, or so I imagined, he certainly had by the time I had met him. I doubted whether Quintus would ever be the same overbearingly muscled and mature Hercules.

To many Quintus would be the more attractive. He was much more the Greek ideal than the young Hercules Burrus had been at that age, but the man was still impressive at forty plus years.

"Don't pump up his head with vanity, gentlemen," Metella said from her spot, her gaze on the boy and her eyes belying her statement. "He is Quintus, that's all. A girl could do worse if she were looking for a husband."

"Hell, Quintus would be a catch for anyone's bed, don't you think, Numer...

"Enough of such talk," snapped Metella eyes flashing with a hardness that would cut marble. "Both of you stop. Keep such masculine indulgences for after dinner when Lucia and I retire. This is not the time for them here.   It is most unsuitable. Now, tell us about the new house, brother. How is the work going?"

"Well, sister. Slowly, but well."

The next few courses were spent talking about plans for the house, the mosaic being laid, the layout of the new garden, and other such trifles. No one was very interested but Metella had taken control of the dinner conversation and not one of us was brave or foolish enough to fight her on it. By the time we had finished the honeyed poppyseed cakes Burrus had gradually slipped more and more in communion with his wine goblet and even Metella had seemed to run out of things to say.

At last the ladies withdrew with a warning for us to not linger long as it was already late. I for one seconded the opinion but knew I'd have to sit through at least one more cup of wine for appearance's sake.

"Very nice," Burrus said leering at the slave girl, Anthia who filled our cups. "Fine young, mare, don't you think Numerius? You know of such things. What do you think of her? From a professional point of view, of course?"

I bit my tongue before answering. Burrus hadn't the sense of propriety to realize that such a comment before his son and his wife's brother at her table was an insult not only to the girl but to his wife as well.

"I think you've had too much wine, my friend." I said as evenly as possible, trying to keep my eyes from him for I could have gladly murdered him on the spot but for the presence of his son, my nephew who appeared embarrassed enough by his father's salaciousness.

"But never too drunk to seal the deal, eh Numerius, and if you have forgotten it, ask your sister. She is a happy woman..." he took another slug of his wine and wiped his mouth with the back of his hand..."by the gods I meant no offence, just pointing out something – Quintus has grown up, Numerius. Just look at the blushes. He knows what I mean about the girl. Already been there or I'm a Greek philosopher. Eh Quintus? Already tried that one , eh? Look, it's okay. I'm your father and I know by the time I was your age not a female slave in the house remained a virgin."

Quintus said nothing but the various shades of red which the countenance of the young man turned sent me wading back into the conversation.

"Boys will be boys, Burrus, as we all know."

"And he's a hell of a young stud."

The boy sputtered his mouthful of wine over the table, choking. I watched astonished as his ears burned brighter red and his father continued unabashed.

Burrus waved a meaty hand at the boy. "You deny it?" he asked. "I tell you, the boy is more like me than you all think, Numerius. Very well equipped is the way I think she put it. Very well indeed. Nothing wrong with that, son. Stop your blushing. Your mother and sister aren't here now, just your Uncle Numerius and me. Don't go getting all flustered like a Vestal in a whorehouse. Be a man."

"I think you've shocked the boy, Burrus." I began trying a smile. "Maybe we should let him keep some of his secrets. We too were young once." Stupid fool, I thought. Burrus would always be the ass I first met all those years ago. "What about your studies? Have you thought anymore on my offer to send you to Greece or are you wanting to get started on your career?" I hoped the question would move us in a new direction.

I knew that Burrus was against the boy's traveling and had said so on numerous occasions, much preferring that the boy go off to some province with one of his own old army comrades. To Burrus, the Greece experience was for women, pathics and "artsy pederasts" as he put it. I would be willing to listen to his nonsense again only to get Quintus off the hook of his father's insensitivity. It didn't work.

"Numerius knows all about studs, eh Numerius?" Burrus cackled and jabbed a big greasy finger in my direction. "He could tell you stories, my boy. By Jupiter, he could tell us all stories."

My gasp caught in my throat. Yes , Burrus knew about some of my past; hell, a lot of Rome knew, but most had the decency not to speak of it. My sister knew only the basics. Burrus, of course, knew more as he had been a small part of it. In the years since the birth of Quintus and Lucia the topic had never been broached among us. I certainly didn't care for the way it was coming up now.

Burrus leered blurry-eyed at the still pink face of Quintus, "Oh, some of the rumors that float around Rome about your Uncle, Quintus. You should..."

I'd had enough. "You...should know they're rumors." I interjected with a harsh laugh. "Rome is full of rumors, has been and always will be." I found myself standing having banged my wine cup onto the table, the rest of the deep amber wine now flowing across the table of dinner debris. "I think I am tired now, Quintus Lucius Burrus, and we've all had too much wine and I think it might be best that we all retire before we go too far."

Burrus glared at me. I was, after all, technically his guest. For a split second I thought he might come across the table at me and for me that would definitely be a losing proposition. He was still a bull of a man and whatever might occur from that point would undoubtedly shatter the tenuous truce that we've balanced so precariously over all these years. What he did, what he said next could easily have changed forever the relationship between him, my sister and her family. I went cold with the possibility of loss. Burrus glared. I could see my nephew's eyes widen.

Burrus stood fists clenched, opened his mouth to speak and out came the loudest belch possible. The gods do have a sense of timing – for a moment we all looked at each other in amazement, then Burrus himself began the laughter – "I'm maybe a little drunk," he said stumbling back a few feet from his couch. "Where are those damn slaves when you need one," he muttered holding onto the table for balance. "Anthia, Castor, help me get to bed," he yelled for the slaves who couldn't have been far as they appeared almost instantly. He threw a heavy arm around their shoulders – still weaving but standing fairly straight now. "Good night, Numerius. Quintus, see your Uncle to his room." He dropped his head, lifted it again, looked into the face of Anthia –"Better get me to bed, sweet thing. I'm going to be sick."

We watched the two slaves stagger off with the weight of their master supported between them.

"He'll be sorry tomorrow,' said Quintus quietly. "He'll also have a hell of a hangover."

"We all will," I smiled.

"Shall I show you to your room?" The boy started in my direction.

"No," I said too strongly and too rapidly. He stopped, a look I couldn't quite place coming over his face. I laughed to cover my unease. "No," that was better, "it's quite all right, my boy. I well know the way, as we all know. Get yourself to bed." I turned and started to the door before he could reply. "I'm off for bed myself. Goodnight."

His voice called his goodnights from behind me. Once out of his sight I moved faster to my rooms. I had sent Aristo to stay the night at the new house with the slaves and furniture. I regretted it and wished I hadn't for now I was agitated and wanted to spew my Burrus' induced venom about the evening onto the reassuring and calming presence of the slave. Aristo would have talked me down. As it was it would take me hours to get to sleep.

I entered the first dark cubicle of my rooms and fumbled for a lamp and flint that was supposed to be on the table. I froze at the sound of movement – the flint was stuck and Apollo stood there lighting the lamp he had been keeping next to him on the couch.

He bowed and offered a wax tablet to me. Holding it to the lamp I read the short and pithy note from Aristo. The slave knew me better than I knew myself.

The gardener stood poised in the lamplight, a freshly scrubbed Adonis with the body of young Hercules, unadorned except for his collar which marked him as property. The look on his face questioned my mood, unsure of whether I was pleased or displeased.

"No, no Apollo. All is well." I sighed and smiled. "Aristo is a very wise man."

Apollo smiled back and set the lamp on the table picking up the cup of my nightly concoction which Aristo had no doubt prepared for me. I downed it with three quick gulps, and thanked the gods for yet one more time that Aristo had come into my life. Apollo for his part, took the empty cup from me, set it back on the table from whence he had retrieved it, and led me to bed.

I woke to Apollo standing over the bed shaking my shoulder. I struggled to sit up and pry my eyes open. "What the hell, Apollo, surely you've..."

The still naked slave made no sound but pointed across to the other room. Andronicus stood there, lamp in hand, a look of disapproval across his brow.

'I'm sorry but you have a messenger, master Numerius. The door keeper didn't know what to do – so he woke me. You have to get up, sir."

"In the morning, Andronicus," I said wanting to roll back over to sleep, my mind numbed by the wine from dinner.

'Now sir," the old man said crossing the space to the bed and holding out to me some sort of sealed message. "It's from the Vestal Pausina."

I sat back up with a jolt. "What? Give it here!"

Andronicus passed me the sealed tablet, his eyes sweeping over the slave but making no verbal comment. "I'll help the master dress, Apollo. You can go back to your room and get some rest. We've plenty of work in the morning." He motioned toward Apollo while he spoke and the boy did as he was instructed grabbing a tunic he'd evidently tucked under the bed. In the dim light I couldn't see if he was embarrassed. I broke the seal while Andronicus held the lamp for me.

Please come immediately – Pausina's very neat stylus had inscribed on the wax. I still recognized her distinctive penmanship. "Well," I said standing. "Andronicus, I have to go down to the center. Are the litter bearers awake?"

"She has sent a closed litter, master. I've sent for a basin of water to freshen yourself. What will you wear?"

And so the old slave helped me prepare for my meeting with the Vestal. I dressed hurriedly but not without care. It had been a long time since Pausina and I had been face to face. I was not prepared to see her in the disheveled and hung over state that Andronicus had found me.

Chapter 3

Rome was sleeping as we made our way though streets recently quieted from the party goers and not yet given over to the early morning people on their way to set up stalls or open shops. The streets of Rome are rarely empty. The carts come and go all evening barred as they are during the day. We worked our way down the Palatine toward the forum, took the turn onto the Via Sacra then on around to the small street which leads behind the Temple and The House of the Vestals. The moonlight lit our way, most of the torches having burnt out by this hour. It was not one of those pitch black nights. Rome stood quiet and ghostly as we passed our way.

Twenty plus years previously I had made   much the same way to Pausina at this very time of the morning; and for a moment I relived those complex feelings of fear and desire that put me in so much   danger   all those years before.   We had been young then, impulsive, and in all probability were drawn to each other more out of a combination of reputation, the thrill of the forbidden, and defiance than any true attraction. We had met through Caligula, that worst of all rulers, who had thought it amusing to present at one of his debauches the boy and girl widely reputed to be the most beautiful in Rome. It didn't matter to him that she was a Vestal and I a slave. Caligula took delight in shocking others, some thought him demented; I thought him cruel, calculating and despicable. From his first days on Capri (where he had been summoned by his Uncle Tiberius) he had taken an almost instant dislike to me and found innumerable ways to harass me on a daily basis. When he came to power he had made my life truly miserable.   I have often asked myself how a slave could attract such hatred and the long term harangue of a man busy ruling the world. It would have been so easy for him just to destroy me.   Instead in some ways he set me up to succeed as I have. I will never understand the man but I hated him and when he died I made a special sacrifice of thanks to those three sisters, goddesses of vengeance.   After that long ago evening of arranged meeting, Pausina and I, in our humiliation had turned to one another. It was natural I suppose that we should form a bond. We began to see each other. I had been nearing sixteen, Pausina even younger, foolish children playing at adult games and laughing at the risks. There were bound to be rumors, and when the fires became hot enough we wisely went our separate ways. The rumors died down and gave way to other rumors either as true or false as the many about each of us. They rarely surface anymore. Rome is a city that thrives on rumors and demands a vast and constant supply of them.

We had circled the temple where inside the sacred flame was kept burning, ensuring the well being of Rome. We made two turns to come in behind the complex and to the back gate of the garden running the length of the house itself. Our journey had been swift and taken me back years. As the litter was lowered just past the gate, I reminded myself that this was the present; those years were gone. I found myself at the opposite end of the garden where I had thought I had seen Pausina earlier in the day. Under moonlight it looked rather dreamlike in its shades of gray and black. I could smell the intoxicating perfume of some night blooming flower with which I was unfamiliar and momentarily wondered if I might ask for a start to carry to the new house.   In the moonlight I could make out some of the various plant specimens which would make welcome additions to ours. I was met and led through the garden to a small wooden door of the house itself. If this meeting went well perhaps we would be able to work our way around to the topic of gardening.

Inside I was led down a brief hallway obviously meant for the household rather than public visitors, storerooms would have been my guess from the smells. The place was quiet, too early for even the kitchen slaves to be up and about. The slave leading me stopped at a door, knocked once and opened it. I entered, and the slave disappeared.

In the light given off by the oil lamps she was still beautiful, older yes, but we all are.

"Numerius Meridius Pulcher, how good of you to come." The formality of her tone surprised me but catching sight of a man standing just to the side of the next doorway, I understood. This was not to be a reunion for talking over old times.

I bowed my head slightly. "And what can I do for the Vestals, Lady?"

"Please. Come with me." She turned leaving me to follow. "This is our physician Aegyptus. I sent for him just before you. He has been here for some time while we waited for you." I started to excuse myself, to make an effort to explain the time delay but she waved it away. "You're here now; follow me." The physician, obviously a Greek, fell in with us. Pausina led us through another doorway and through the darkness of what was obviously the kitchen proper then down two corridors where she stopped before a heavy wooden door.

"We have a problem," she said turning to face me. What you see must be kept quiet. You agree?"

"Of course, Lady," I said before she turned back and opened the door. The physician said nothing, but I figured he'd been warned before my arrival.

The room we entered was luxurious if not overly ornate, the subdued luxury one would expect to surround the Vestals. I knew it to be the private rooms of a Vestal as I had occasion to visit similar rooms many years ago. Pausina walked straight from the sitting room to the curtained off bedroom. "Here it is" she said pulling the curtain aside and exposing the naked and bloody body of a very attractive young woman. "Laelia," Pausina said and for a moment it sounded as if her voice would crack. "We found her in the garden wrapped up in that." She pointed to the toga thrown carelessly on the floor, it too soaked in blood. "We need your help, Numerius Meridius."

I nodded, my mind already racing. "She's a ..."

"A Vestal," said Pausina firmly. "A very good one, one that I had hoped might one day soon take my place. I will retire next spring and she was the one...She was... special to me and now this."

I stepped closer to the bed, a bloody mess. Then it hit me. Yes, the head lay all wrong on the pillow. Her neck had been snapped and the blood appeared nowhere above … Venus on a stick, I thought appalled. Pausina nodded "Yes, Aegyptus has already assured us that she has given birth. You see why we must keep it quiet . The child was nowhere to be found. Will you help us Numerius? Will you help me?"

"I nodded my head slowly. Of course I will, Lady." I leaned over the bed to get a closer look in the dim lighting. At least the girl was dead – at least she had escaped the fate the law would have demanded of her had she been found out. I turned to Pausina "How do you hide a pregnant Vestal let alone a child in the House of the Vestals?"

Pausina sighed with something between irritation and resolution. She sat on the edge of the bed to wipe the wisps of hair from the girl's face. "She was special, Numerius."

I lifted the bloodied toga from the floor. Something fell, the sound shattering across the marble floor and coming to a stop just under the bed. It was a necklace, a child's necklace, obviously a bulla worn by a child for luck and protection and far too large for a baby. Under closer scrutiny by the light of the lamp the bulla proved to be gold, fine work, either an antique piece or a good reproduction. Whichever, it had cost a pretty piece or two. A gift? How had it become wrapped up in the toga? The toga itself raised other questions, Roman men wore togas and Roman prostitutes. His or hers? A disguise or something to cover the deed? On the small table next to the bed lay a spent flower bloom no doubt picked from the garden as I recalled passing a bank of them moments ago, also a small glass vial. Picking that up, I pulled the stopper and was immediately rewarded with the wonderful scent of a Persian perfume, rare and expensive.

"It was her favorite," Pausina said acknowledging the smell.

"Expensive."

A small vanity, Numerius Meridius," Pausina said with a smile. "Even a vestal wants to feel as if she is still desirable. We have taken no vow of poverty. Besides, I believe they were gifts."

"They?" I raised an eyebrow and for the briefest of moments Pausina looked as if she'd made a mistake.

"Well, I mean she'd been wearing that particular concoction for nearly a year. There must have been more than one vial don't you think? You're familiar with perfumes, Numerius. A vial that size doesn't last forever."

"No, it wouldn't," I said covering the quick mental thought about why Pausina had both made it a slight admonition and used the familiar form of my name in front of the physician. It was unlike

Pausina to be careless. I looked at the physician and back at Pausina with a quick raise of an eyebrow.

"No," she answered. "Aegyptus is to be trusted. You can say anything you would say to me in front of him." I nodded but, doubted if it were true, or that she had meant for me to believe it.

"I guess there's no point in asking who might have done this. Who she was seeing outside of the House? Who the father of the baby might be? Who's been trying to see her?"

The Physician looked at Pausina and Pausina looked at me. "No. We've no idea."

Well I had to ask. "And no one knew she was pregnant?" Again the chain of physician to Pausina and on to me. This time something in the physician's eyes told me the answer to this one.

Pausina looked at me calmly. "I would prefer not to answer that one, Numerius Meridius."

"You don't have to." I could only assume she wanted to be able to vow that such a thing had never been spoken of.

"We take care of our own, Numerius Pulcher."

"Enemies in the House?"

"None"

"Friends?"

"None."

"You're being very helpful here. Where's her slave girl? Surely she had one and they always know more about their Mistresses than the Mistress herself."

"Gone."

"Gone?"

"Gone."

"Gone or missing?" I was beginning to feel as if I were swimming upstream.

"Missing."

The one word answers were starting to ruffle my feathers. "You're not being too helpful here, Pausina."

"Sorry." Her voice was calm, flat and final. I wouldn't be getting more from her. Nothing like being asked to help out and then cut off. I looked over at Aegyptus – "Well, about how long ago did she have the baby? Surely you can tell me that." The physician looked once again at Pausina. "Oh for the love of the Jove, just tell me and stop looking at her to give your answers." I'd had enough of that charade.

"He can't."

"He's a physician isn't he?"

"Mute."

"A mute physician? That must be useful."

"We've learned to communicate, Numerius. He has served us well over the years. You are not to give Aegyptus grief. Anything you want to ask you may ask through me." She looked at me, her expression firm.

"Well,..." I began to repeat the question.

"It must have been within a couple of hours of our finding her. And that was two hours before I sent for you both while I was deciding who to call on and then where to find you."

"Who found her?"

"Her slave, Chloe."

"And now she's missing?

"Yes."

I did a quick calculation. Two, four, one for me to get here – so about five to six hours previously, about the time Burrus, Quintus and I had been finishing dinner.

"So, what is it you want from me, Pausina? Exactly what am I supposed to do?"

"Find out who did this and find out what has happened to the baby." She stopped me from interrupting with two fingers held upward. Her years as chief Vestal had given her a real boost of natural authority; but even as a young girl she had given occasional displays of it. "That is it, Numerius. Find out and tell me. Nothing else." She stressed the simple statement. "For reasons that have to do with this house and thereby with the welfare of Rome no one else must know of this. I will take care of the justice side of the matter; from you I want only information and your promise of silence."

"Discretion has always been my strong suit."

"Which is why I have you standing here."

"Then three things, Lady. First, tell me about her slave. Second, tell me about the lady herself and third, tell me..."

"And so I will, Numerius. Come to my rooms for a cup of wine if you have seen what you want here. It's early, but after all of this I need something more fortifying than fruit juice. Aegyptus, take care of her. I'll be back when Numerius Meridius has gone and that must be before daylight."

She led me through a warren of rooms public and private until we came to her own private apartments where she poured us both a bracing cup of wine and we settled down to talk more openly.

"I'm sure you realize, Numerius, how important it is that we keep all of this a secret. Public scandal would benefit no one, and as for the girl, well she's already paid the price, hasn't she? I would prefer her family not have to suffer the disgrace that public knowledge of the thing would entail. They're a good and noble family. I would hate to see them injured unduly."

I noticed she said nothing about the damage it would do to the reputation of the house and the Vestals, but said nothing about the oversight.

"And your physician has been caring for the girl? Did he deliver the child?"

"Aegyptus? Certainly not. I suspect Chloe was there for that. She should have come to me and we wouldn't be in this mess. She'll have quite a bit to answer for when she's located. I want her and the baby found, Numerius. That's important to me. Chloe, the baby and whoever did this. All I want is for you to provide me with the information. Be very clear on that. Take no action yourself, tell no one else, just the information. I'll take care of it from there. All I want from you are the players and the facts. You will leave the rest to me. Now, we both know you're good at finding out things. Find them for me, Numerius. For old times sake if nothing else. You will do that for me, won't you? I'd like to put this behind us before I step down next spring. I'm tired and ready to retire from public life. I've done my duty to the goddess and to Rome. I'm looking forward to living out the quiet life at one of my villas." She drained her cup and set it down on a richly carved table.

"Retirement has its benefits, although I never took you for one to give all of this up, Pausina," I said putting my thoughts into words, for I did in fact find it hard to believe.

She looked away from me and around the luxuriously appointed room. "Oh, it has been a good life. I don't deny that, but I've put in my thirty years, Numerius. I'm tired. I deserve to live the remainder of my life as I see fit, for me and for no one else. I want to experience the normal life I once knew as a little girl, before I came to this place. I have grown weary of the power and the ritual. I am merely another woman after all." She smiled, somewhat cynically perhaps, but somewhere there was an element of truth to it all no doubt.

She gave me little more to go on. We turned to talking about the past, our present and things of little importance. I'd been right that the good physician wasn't privy to quite everything, and certainly not to our past history. She trusted him no doubt and I suspected from the way she talked about him that he might serve as more than a mere physician; but there was a place where the door of trust slammed closed. Pausina had been too powerful too long to fully trust anyone. That included me, although she didn't say it. A woman with the history and position of Pausina had had to walk a complex and circuitous path to arrive where she was. It was not easy to survive at the top in Rome. I certainly understood that from my own life and I had never had the power nor the public scrutiny that comes with such power. I had merely been famous for being infamous, for consorting with the rich and powerful and the famous.

It was a precarious walk. It hardened you and made it difficult to trust. True friends became hard to find, utter trust in one of them almost impossible.

Back in the garden she sent me on my way. I left her, wanting to give her the benefit of the doubt, but a part of me was certain she knew more than she was sharing with me.

Chapter 4

I left the Vestal's garden in a different litter than the one I had arrived in, far less luxurious but I chose to believe that was because of Pausina's desire for it to blend in with the early morning traffic rather than any subtle comment on our meeting.   The ride back up to the Palatine came just as the sun was breaking. It was still early for most traffic but already the streets were busy with those who opened early, the markets, vendors, shop owners and the other miscellaneous men, women, freedmen and slaves that get our city ready for a day's business.

Aristo met me at the door with Andronicus standing at his side looking vaguely put out.   Slaves don't like other slaves interfering in their carefully delineated duties. The door belonged to Andronicus, the presence of Aristo there was tolerated by the old man entirely out of respect for me and Aristo's standing as my personal and favored slave. Andronicus would never have tolerated another slave's hovering over his domain.

"Your breakfast is waiting in your rooms." Aristo said quietly and I saw the look of relief on his face. He asked no questions but raised an eyebrow.

"Good, Come with. We need to talk. Thank you, Andronicus. As you see I have returned safely. You did the right thing getting me up earlier. Thank you, again." I smiled at the old man and watched him shuffle off to his other morning chores.   "Now, for that breakfast," I said to Aristo unfastening my mantle.

Aristo bowed, took the offered mantle and followed me through the house to my room. There on the table lay the fresh fruit and olives that I prefer for breakfast. As I lay on the couch he deftly cut the fruit into manageable slices and arranged them on the plate.

"We've got a game to play," I said over the rim of my morning brew – some nasty flavored herbal concoction I had started drinking back in the day of the Old Tiberius. I've grown used to the slightly sticky consistency and the bitter bite the base herb gives this concoction meant to keep me healthy and who I am. Even so, I've thought of giving it up, but unsure of where that might lead, I never do it.

"You have only just arrived here." Aristo said a note of disapproval in his voice. "There is much to be done with the new house and all." He placed the plate of fruits in front of me and sat in the nearby chair. "So, tell me."

"Very heady stuff. Probably one for my books," I said. Aristo rolled his eyes but said nothing. At that time I was always talking of writing down my adventures. Never quite got around to doing it but I was constantly threatening to. Aristo vacillated between disbelief and the half-hearted hope that I would one day give up my adventures and take us somewhere quiet to write about them. That way he would finally have me safe and sound and much more securely under his vigilant care.

"So tell me," he repeated.

"A Vestal's been killed. Murdered. A Vestal who had just given birth, no less."

"A pregnant Vestal? How in the world of Hades...?"

"Not pregnant, having given birth, and the infant nowhere to be found. I've got to find that baby, Aristo. I must find the baby and the man who is responsible."

"For the baby or the murder?"

"Probably both, don't you think? There's a good chance the father is the murderer. I mean if he wanted the little thing and she didn't want to give it up... well, you know the penalties for messing with a Vestal. He probably has an aversion to horrible deaths. Yes, probably one and the same man, lover, father and murderer. Welcome back to Rome."

"And just how did you stumble upon this fine mess? One night in Rome, you were supposed to be here with your family, safe and sound. Why did you go out? Couldn't you just stay still one night..."

I cut him off. "Oh no, I was indeed here and behaving myself, quite well under the circumstances but more on that mess later. I was summoned."

"Summoned?"

"Yes, by the Vestal Pausina. The chief Vestal herself." I saw his eyes tighten. "No, now don't go rushing down that road, my man. Ancient history and over rumored. There's nothing to this at all except a simple case of murder and missing child. Period!"

"That's what you always say and it never is simple and there's always 'something' to it."

"I shook my head emphatically and picked up a few more of the olives from the plate. "Not this time my friend. On the great thigh of Jupiter, I vow it."

"Don't make vows in jest. One day the gods may catch up with you."

"Haven't yet. Besides they owe me."

He tried to look stern but I could tell he was coming around. Slave or not it was always best to have Aristo on my side in these things.

"So here we go. Ready? To Do: Find and talk to Chloe, the girl's slave. Talk to brother and or her family if the brother won't help... Looking for: lover, friends, foes, jealousies, secrets. That's a start. Pausina doesn't want me to talk to the other Vestals yet. She'll only allow it if it is absolutely necessary. Understandable, considering we're dealing with a fallen Vestal. The slaves she can arrange for me to meet. The family of the girl lives up on the Quirinal not far from the new house. The brother, a Marcus Flavius, seems to be the family member who visits most. Let's start with him. Chloe will be a harder nut to crack as she's temporarily disappeared, but we might try other slaves and the markets where she and Laelia, that's the girl's name, shopped. Pausina gave me the name of a perfumery shop that the girl was partial to."

Aristo was busy scribbling away while I talked. One of his most useful talents was the shorthand that Cicero's Tiro had come up with. It was surprisingly quick and difficult to decipher for the untrained. Aristo was a master at it having picked up the study of it when we were still at the Golden Wing. At the time, I was desperately trying to find reasons not to put him to the work of that place. "Oh yes, that reminds me. I thought we might pay a visit to Hesperia as well."

Aristo looked up to flash a smile of approval. Hesperia was the closest thing he had to a mother, or maybe a big sister. The two have always doted on one another, and with Hesperia that was saying something, but she had taken him under her wing from the moment he had arrived at the Golden Wing. Later I suspected that it had been her plan all along to transfer him safely from under her wing to under mine. I was never quite sure and she denies it to this day, but Hesperia can be very convincing when she has a plan.

"The Quirinal first, then Hesperia on the way back. The markets and perfumery will have to wait until afternoon or tomorrow. Right now, I desire a bath and something to wear that will not totally shock the Flavii but will still raise a lot of envy on the part of Hesperia. Think you can manage that?" I popped the last olive into my mouth and pushed away the empty plate.

"Greek, Roman, Phoenician or maybe that mauve silk from Armenia?" Aristo, stood to put his writing stuff neatly away.

"Maybe a bit much for the Flavii; remember they'll be in mourning. Let's do Roman and concentrate on some accessories that'll get Hesperia going."

"Toga Roman?"

"No. No reason to go that far – tunic and mantle. That'll do it nicely. Maybe the buttery tunic from Egypt and the Coan silk mantle? Yes, that should do it. Did we bring the ocher and gold worked sandals? Those should light up her eyes. And the topaz stones. Simple cuffs. Maybe the antique Greek beaten gold ones, those should open her eyes up."

Aristo grinned. "You are cruel."

'Maybe a little, but I worked for it. Let her see where she might get if she plays her cards wisely and works as hard as I did at it."

Aristo chuckled as I kicked out of the simple tunic I'd put on this morning and left it in a heap on the floor. One nice thing about having slaves; they do the picking up. "Where's the bath?"

"I had them put it in the bedroom."

"Good." I started to move in that direction then turned back as he stooped to pick up the discarded tunic. "By the way, about that gardener?"

"He raised his eyes. "Yes."

"Very thoughtful of you."

He smiled and shook his head. "Even a one nighter deserves his chance." "You did well to give him his chance." Aristo is an uncommon slave, slave and friend. And although he would never ask for acknowledgement, I knew it was important to him.

Chapter 5

The house of the Flavii was on the Quirinal Hill not far from my own. It was of newer construction but built in the old style, solidly Roman with the prerequisite austerity but with more embellishment than one would find in the old houses of the Palatine. The slave that opened the heavy wooden door was in mourning and stood momentarily agape at my presence. Granted I am not what one usually expects to find on the other side of a knock on a respectable Roman home's door. I have never adhered to the Roman penchant for short hair, and my taste in clothing definitely leans toward the Eastern styling. The poor man probably thought an Eastern Ambassador had shown up by mistake – or maybe shown up early for a fancy dress dinner party no one had told him about; or more likely, that someone had ordered up something from an exotic brothel. Still, give the fellow his due, he quickly recovered and asked us our business.

When we asked to see the young master Marcus Flavius, the slave looked at us warily, nodded curtly and shut the door with a muttered instruction to wait a moment. We heard the bolt slide in place. "Maybe I overdressed," I grinned at Aristo. We were used to it.

The door was reopened in short order. The same slave with only a hint of disgust ushered us across the threshold and into the atrium. "The master will be with you shortly," he said taking up a position by one of the doors, obviously thinking that these were not the type of visitors to be left on their own, even momentarily. He stood at the doorway, arms crossed, looking down his long Greek nose at us, letting us know without a word that we were definitely not of the stuff he was accustomed to admitting through the front entrance of this house. I glanced at Aristo who comfortably ignored the fellow by staring right past him. As for me, I took the time to investigate the mural of the Romulus and Remus . Adequately done, but rather subdued and with no artistic flair. Like the house, the decoration was solidly Roman without surprises. Money without taste is a disappointment. Too much money coupled with bad taste is a crime. Here, in this house, it was merely the former.

I heard the man's approach before he actually appeared, the sandals slapping industriously on the marbled floor.

"Ah, sorry to keep..." He stopped both physically and vocally just inside the doorway. It had only been for a split second but it was an obvious gap that none present could fail to notice.

"I understand you wish to see Marcus," he said carefully flicking his toga higher on his arm. "I am Marcus Flavius Camillus, his father. I am inclined to ask what this is about and if it is absolutely necessary. Marcus is in his room. We are in mourning, unfortunately. Just this morning in fact. May I ask your business?"

He was an old Roman indeed meeting callers in a toga. Well into his fifties I guessed, a prim and proper Roman paterfamilias. His thinning body and hair aged him but he was still in such shape as to hint at the attractive young Roman he must once have been. Did I know him?

"I am Numerius Meridius Pulcher, and yes, we have already heard of your loss. Our condolences, Marcus Flavius. Actually, it was Pausina who suggested we visit and talk to your son."

"Pausina?" The man sounded astonished. Then, as some inward cog of his mind slipped into place, his face changed. "Oh, you are the man she said would be investigating...sorry, I just didn't expect you to ...to...," he stuttered to a stop.

I was suddenly sure I knew the man from somewhere. "To be quite as we are?" I said with my best smile. "No we're not your typical investigators, I admit. Think nothing of it. Aristo and I are quite used to it. We would however like to talk to young Marcus if at all possible. I understand he visited your daughter quite often. "

"Just yesterday as a matter of fact. He was the last of the family to see her. Let me get him for you. Larchis, take the gentlemen to my study. I will send Marcus to them."

For a moment Larchis shot a look at Old Marcus as if he'd gone quite mad. This obviously was not normal procedure but like any well-trained slave he recovered almost immediately, stepping forward with a half bow and indicating the doorway where he stood and said "This way gentlemen," with only the slightest note of disdain on the last of the words. Old Marcus had already disappeared. For someone who had intercepted our visit to his son he had beaten a hasty retreat. What might that be about? Of course I had seen and been seen by many men during my years in Rome. There was no way to remember them all.

We were ushered into a sizable study which, like the rest of the house, expressed the good Roman standard avoiding any hint of unnecessary luxury. It was neat and tidy but obviously a working study not like so many Roman houses just for show. I used the time to examine the wall of cubbies stashed neatly with their carefully labeled hanging tags for easy identification. Science, Farming, Army. Nothing exciting here, let alone provocative. Old Marcus Flavius was no doubt as straight an arrow as they came in those days.

Young Marcus was nothing like his father. With the younger Flavius' entrance the entire energy in the room changed. "My father said you wished to see me." He was a young man of easy fashion even in his mourning clothes. Fancy haircut, nails minutely cared for and simply an air about him that screamed youth, energy, and conviviality. Very unlike his father. I noted the resemblance to the dead girl instantly though. The two could have been twins, the same coloring of hair and eyes, the same fine features. Judging from their father's attractive but rather pedestrian look, the siblings must have taken after their mother, and she had to be a looker.

"You must be Numerius Meridius Pulcher. I am honored to meet you." Marcus crossed the floor extending his hand; it was not a reaction I often encountered in the houses of Rome's patricians, or, for that matter, in public in general.

"Marcus Flavius, I regret having to interfere..."

"Oh, do call me Marcus, and I'll call you Numerius if you don't mind. Although I certainly see how the Pulcher fits. Jupiter, I must sound like the perfect fool, but I've already heard so much about you. I'm a friend of young Quintus. He's told us the most wonderful stories about you and your days in Rome.   All quite tasteful mind you -- none of the rumors that -- well, he thinks very highly of you."

"And I of him."

"Come let's sit down. Can I send for some wine? We have a rather good vintage from our farm in Alba Fucens. Please," he said indicating the couch at the end of the room.

"This chair will do fine," I said and sat myself in one of the two chairs facing the couch. I tried to suppress a smile. The little thing was flirting with me, charming but half my age and rather clumsy about it.

"Your man there can hang out in kitchen while we talk. I'm sure they'll find some refreshment for him as well. This way," He looked briefly up and down Aristo who was none too happy. "Come, I'll show you the way and order our wine at the same time."

He led the way and Aristo followed but not before casting a scowl over his shoulder toward me. I waved him on and sat back in the chair. Maybe Aristo would find some entertainment of his own in the kitchens and regardless of that, it would give him a chance to see what the slaves of the household might know and they usually know much more than their masters think. I also wondered just what Quintus had been telling his friends about me. I had always imagined I was the black sheep that the family would prefer not to mention outside the household, a family "secret" in so far as one is able to keep a secret in Rome. The fact that Quintus evidently was regaling his friends with stories about me was somewhat amusing to me. Still, it certainly was not the reception I had expected from Young Flavius, especially under the circumstances.

When he returned, still all smiles, Flavius draped himself rather conspicuously over the couch. "The wine is coming momentarily and then we'll be able to talk in utter privacy," he said. "You're quite comfortable in that chair? The room's a bit stuffy. If you'd rather, my rooms are a bit more comfortable and..."

"Here is fine, Marcus Flavius." I said in my best schoolmaster tone. "I need to ask you a few questions."

"Ah, but surely you'll call me Marcus. Please. I'll answer your questions but only on the condition you call me my Marcus. Agreed?" He smiled a smile that rivaled starlight, a natural born flirt.

"Agreed."

"And, on the condition I can call you Numerius. Agreed?" Again the smile.

A slave entering with our wine saved me from having to answer him. The pretty young girl offered me the first cup from the tray and then proceeded to her young master.

"Thank you, Europa" Marcus Flavius smiled at the girl. "That will be all except tell old Larchis to see that we're not disturbed. " He flashed another smile at the girl every bit as bright as the one directed at me, and she received it with obvious pleasure. He was the consummate little flirt, or maybe it was just his nature.

"Pretty thing," I said when the girl had gone. The wine was unusually good, as few home grown vintages are despite what their owners believe.

"Europa? Oh yes, she's very pretty, but a little on the naïve side."

"Hmm," I murmured and took another sip of the wine. One thing slaves in Rome were not was naïve. At least, not by the time they had reached the girl's age which I calculated to be about sixteen. I'm a good judge of ages, comes with my past business. I decided to ignore the remark and its implication. I was, after all, here on business. "So, what can you tell me about your sister that might help me? You were close I understand? I hear you visited quite often."

He grew more serious. "Someone had to see that she had some fun, caught up in that dreadfully dull place. Have you ever been to the House of the Vestals?"

"Indeed I have. I have the highest regard for the ladies there. They are providing a sacred service. It is an ancient and honorable position in Rome, as you well know. There aren't many higher positions for a woman."

"Well, Laelia hated it," he said unimpressed with my obvious statement of the Roman line of Honor and Glory for the sake of

Rome.   "How Father and Mother could have allowed it I'll never understand. Laelia was meant to be free with a life of parties and fun and laughter. She was that way even as a child. How they even considered putting her there is beyond me. Except that Father might have thought it protection."

"Protection?"

"From herself, Laelia was very much a free spirit and he's... well... very stiff as you surely noticed.   Father certainly doesn't approve of fun...or much else as a matter of fact. He nearly flipped his toga when he saw you. Muttered something to me about talking to you and ran off to hide somewhere. At least that's the impression I got."

"I have that effect on people sometimes," I said.

"I think you're wonderful." He sat his wine cup down and struck what was meant to be a suggestive pose. He would have gone far in my old business but he lacked finesse.

"Back to your sister," I said tiring of the game.   "I need information, Marcus.   We can talk another time, perhaps with Quintus, if you want to know more about me. The stories and the rumors by the way are wildly exaggerated.   Right now I need answers."   I used my best stern uncle's voice and it had effect. Flavius sat upright and for a moment I wasn't sure whether he would rise in anger or give me what I wanted. He decided against the anger.

"So what do you want to know, Numerius?" The game was over. I was free to go on, at least temporarily.

"Just how much do you know about all of this?"

"Nothing really," he said rather too innocently. "I merely visited her every few days, when her schedule allowed it. You know, to take her out a bit, to have a bit of fun. I thought she deserved it, Numerius. You should be able to understand how a life like that can imprison you. I just intended for her to have some fun."

"So, who was the father of the baby? Surely you know or have a good guess." I went straight to it, hoping to catch him off guard.

His eyes widened, perhaps a bit too wide. "That's impossible; she was a Vestal after all. I can't believe that, Numerius. Surely I would have known that."

"My thought exactly, after all you saw her only yesterday."

"No, no Numerius, you have to believe me," he fumbled badly. "I mean, I saw her yesterday, but I had no idea...that...that such a thing was possible. Really."

"You couldn't see that she was pregnant? That she was about to give birth?"

"No, I swear it. Come to think of it, I can see why."

"Why what?"

"Why I didn't notice. The last few times I've seen her she's always had herself wrapped up in a monstrous cloak of some kind."

"You didn't find that odd in this weather?"

"She said she was cold, I never really questioned it. Besides when we went out, she didn't like to be recognized. She often covered up completely."

"So you did take her out and about?" I asked with the growing suspicion that he knew exactly who the father was and may even have played some kind of role in the affair itself.

"Just shopping and such, little day trips to amuse her."

"No introductions? No excursions with friends?"

"Certainly not, Numerius. Whatever do you take me for?" He stood up in protest, again overplayed.

"A loving brother who thought he would make her life easier to bear. That's what I take you for, Marcus. I thank you for your time, but I can see no reason to proceed at this point. If you would be so good as to send for my man, we'll be off." It was the best I would do at the moment; time to withdraw. I would meet up with Marcus Flavius another time. I had had enough for the moment.

We said our goodbyes and Aristo was sent for.

"Well?" asked Aristo when we were safely back in the litter and headed back down to the center.

"He obviously cared a great deal for his sister and evidently was closer to her than either the father or the mother. Thinks the Old Man is a heartless fool, noncommittal on the Mother. Still he swears he didn't know about the pregnancy and even that he had no idea that she has been with a man. Both are lies; that much I am sure of. He's the one that escorted her out of the house and about. He knows the man, probably set up the introduction; and, even if he didn't know about the when, where, and wherefores of the pregnancy, there's no way he could have missed it yesterday, now is there? His explanation is that when he saw her she was wearing a cloak, must have been some cloak, don't you think? Young Marcus knows a whole lot more than he's saying, but he's not quite ready to tell."

"Ditto from the kitchen," Aristo nodded. "He visited his sister quite a bit, hates the old man. The mother is largely ignored. Quite the partier about town though, is said to mount anything that moves and isn't totally unattractive. Lies through his teeth; isn't so much stupid as thoughtless. Constantly tries to ruffle the feathers of the old man. And he was out much later than usual last night, returning near dawn and stinking of horse. Mother and Father in all evening. Separate but at home. Quite a bit of that lately or so my sources say."

"My, you have done well." What Aristo could get from the slaves of a household often far outstripped what I could get from their disingenuous masters.

"Yes, it's surprising what high praise for the talents of a cook can do, especially when they're sprinkled with a promising smile and a well placed pat here and there." He grinned at me. I wasn't the only one who knew how to use his charms. "However you may rest assured I still have my honor intact. Cassia was far too busy to take a break, but we've an opening for the future if need be."

"Good job. And your take on our boy?"

Aristo's grin flattened. "Pompous little pup. Watch the slimy little bugger. He'll ooze all over you if he gets the chance. I wouldn't believe him if he swore with his hand on the altar of Jupiter. "

"Yes – he did spread it a bit thick. I'll give you that. Pushy and far too caught up in himself."

Aristo spat. "Little rooster. I've seen more subtlety with whores at the Golden Wing. Surely you won't fall for his act."

I smiled. "You needn't worry Aristo. I've been around the track once or twice myself. You too can rest assured my honor is still intact where young Marcus is concerned and will remain so."

"And the father, now he was something. What did you think about the old guy. Didn't you think his behavior odd?"

"Yes ," I nodded, "Odd, indeed. His obvious intention at first was to cut us off from seeing the son. Then he suddenly took flight. Something made him quite nervous. Even the boy mentioned it. I'll have to think about that one, but as far as the young Marcus goes, although he's definitely lying about what he knows, I can't see him as the irate brother killing his sister out of stained family honor."

Aristo snorted. "I doubt he knows the meaning of the word, but I wouldn't put much else beyond him."

"Well, at least that's something. As for the other bits, we'll have another chance. Turns out the boy is friends with Quintus and I've planted the idea that we should all get together for a night of storytelling regarding my infamous past."

'I just bet he'll jump on that one."

"Ah, be kind, Aristo. He's a curious youth. You can't blame him for that."

Aristo folded his arms. "Can and do." He can be adamant when he takes a dislike to someone.

"Anyway, I want to stop at that perfume shop if we can find it. Pick up something for Hesperia and see what else we might find out."

"We can find it." Aristo leaned briefly out of the litter to give directions then settled back onto the cushions. "Who would kill a Vestal?"

"Someone with more to lose than their fear of divine retribution."

"That certainly limits the field doesn't it?"

"Don't be so sarcastic, my man. There are plenty of Romans who truly believe."

"When it's convenient."

"Cynic."

"If you say so."

"Ah, and I'm supposed to be the jaded one. Careful ,Aristo, you may end up shocking me yet. Did we bring anything to drink? I'm suddenly parched."

Chapter 6

The perfume shop was top rate, with prices to match. If our reception at the house of the Flavii had been less than magnanimous, our presence at the door of the shop was more than appreciated. The owner himself brushed aside the extravagantly groomed slaves who dealt with the usual customers. The owner was a good judge of money and must have detected at first glance that here was someone willing to spend major funds on scent. No doubt my penchant for over-indulging in jewels and fine fabric gave him that impression.

"Enter, enter gentlemen. And what are we searching for today?" The tone was as annoying as it was ingratiating. "We have the finest scents in all Rome." His eyes swept over me deftly adding up the cost of everything I wore. "Oils, we have the best; attar of roses, crocus, ointments and dry, lotions that erase time." I arched my brow sharply. He quickly backed away in an attempt at recovery. "Not that there is a need for them, of course. Still one is never too young to start a daily regimen to guard against the future. My name is Hermogines. Welcome to my shop and how may I help you gentlemen today?" He came to a sudden halt; took a deep breath and his eyes widened..." My! Correct me if I'm wrong but that is Spikenard is it not?" He took another sniff. "Indian Nard, Attar from the Valerian of the Indus. Oh, no doubt about it; it is heavenly. And we carry it; indeed we do, when we can get it, a true connoisseur's scent, gentlemen." The man knew his perfumes that I'd give him despite his puffed up delivery. And for what this scent sold it was no wonder that his eyes were sparkling. "Come, come. A cup of wine or perhaps some refreshing fruit juices? Please, sit in our savor room. I will show you Rome's finest, absolutely the finest, scents money can buy." I thought I'd choke on the savor room bit and I knew Aristo would be gagging already, but I nodded and allowed us to be ushered into a heavily curtained off alcove that would have done the Golden

Wing proud. I sat and Aristo stood directly behind me assuming his most solid and detached posture.

Hermogines' eyes took it all in. Having tallied me up earlier he let those same sharp assessing eyes slide quickly over my slave. He liked what he saw. "And what can I do for you today? Looking for more of the Indian? It can be so difficult to find but I do have some similar. Or perhaps something new and different? I have a lovely mix fresh from the east, truly magnificent, like a walk through a moonlit garden…"

I wonder if old H ever let his customers get a word in edgewise. The way he was going on, he'd be well advised to let the slaves do the selling. "A gift. I'm looking for a rather special gift…" I saw his eyes flit quickly over Aristo trying to judge whether he was the special recipient to be or just a regular slave. I decided to let him step in it.

"Oh," he paused unsure. I grinned and he went on. "Of course I have various mixtures, mixtures for every taste, and every sort of person, refined, manly." He cast his eyes at Aristo. "Fresh, clean, manly scents from the mountains. Not all perfumes are heavy and sweet; we have a wide selection."

Although amusing I decided to put an end to his babbling. "No, no it's for a lady. A lady friend who likes it… how shall I say, refined but not too subtle. No, let's make that expensive and not at all subtle."

Hermogines crinkled his nose. "Of course, like I said we have scents for all tastes. Ahem, here are the refreshments, excuse me and enjoy while I pull a few samples. I'll be right back, gentlemen."

"You have an admirer, Aristo." I teased picking out a cup of some fruit juice concoction in a lovely colored glass tumbler. "The shop must be doing well indeed."

"Spare me." Aristo snorted. "Just buy the stuff, ask the questions needed to be asked and get me out of here as quickly as possible. The smells alone are giving me a headache."

"Rather too pungent for your tastes?"

" It smells like a whore house in here."

"Tch, Tch, now."

"A cheap whore house."

"Nothing cheap about it Aristo.."

"I said cheap not inexpensive."

'Such a stickler Aristo." He set his jaw and went silent on me.

Hermogines reentered with a tray of several sample vials which he went over in excruciating detail even for me. I can only imagine the effect on Aristo. I made a mental note not to ask.

Finally we selected, old H and I, a rich lilly infused oil which he assured us came all the way from Arabias. Hesperia would like it and my guess would be that it'd fill any room she walked through. As I said earlier, she wasn't exactly the subtle type. After I had picked the scent and the quantity, we haggled only briefly on the price.

"As for the container," began Hermogines, "What did we have in mind?"

I waved a hand, "Oh something expensive with flash, lots of flash and she likes pink."

"I have just the thing; shall I show it to you?"

"No. I'll trust you. Just wrap it up. Oh, and one more thing, I have one other item." I looked up at Aristo as he dug out of his purse the vial of perfume I had taken from the Vestal's room and transferred to another vial that the proprietor would not recognize. "It's for another friend. Do you know it?"

Once again I had to credit old H.   on his discriminating nose.   He took the vial, removed the stopper and sniffed. "Oh yes, it's a wonderful choice indeed. A marvelous Greek blend of cassia, cinnamon and myrrh...Megaleion, one of the finest. It's very distinctive, truly lovely. And yes we carry it, one of the few in Rome who do, I should think.   I have regulars for this one. Perhaps I know your friend."

I smiled. "Oh I doubt it, this lady is from Pompeii. Rufilla rarely gets to Rome." I made up the name on the spot. It was as good as any.

"Oh well, if the lady ever needs a supply we could have it sent to her."

"Well let me take some now. About the same amount as the other, and in something nice but rather on the simple side. Rufilla is not your flashy type."

"Of course not, "Hermogines replied. "Not with this scent. I have three customers who buy it on a regular basis, all very refined."

"Really?" I asked when it appeared he had finished.

"Oh yes, there is an older lady of quite the high rank, Faustina Lepidus, up on the Viminal and a young man, who no doubt buys it for his lady love and an extremely well spoken slave girl whose Mistress sends her for it on a fairly regular basis. And from my judgment of the slave girl, the lady must be well positioned."

"A young man you say? It really seems an odd choice for a young man, don't you think? What young man would be so..." I let it hang hoping he'd fill in the blank and continue.

"Discriminating? Well, the young Quintus is no doubt very refined, but I would imagine he was told by the lady. He walked in and asked for it by name."

"Quintus? Not Quintus Lucius by any chance, from over on the Palatine?" I sat up hoping not to look too surprised although the name had hit me in the gut.

"No, no. Young Quintus Aronius from out on the Janiculum. We've delivered it out there several times and quite a place it is. He always orders the same. He must be quite fond of the lady."

"Well, he sounds like a good one. I suggest the lady keep hold of him." I stood. "Aristo will pay you. Wrap it all up and give them to him. I'll wait in the litter."

"Oh, no trouble at all," Hermogines said following me toward the door. "Come back when you have a need for anything, anything, at all. I always have something new and exciting."

"I will. It's always good to know a shop in Rome. We'll be back before we leave town. I can assure you of that."

"Any time, any time..." he bowed and scraped me out.

For my part I took a breath of fresh Rome air and climbed into the litter to wait patiently for Aristo in peace and quiet. It took more than a little while and I could only imagine the grilling poor Aristo must be getting from old H. He would not be pleased.

The purple face when Aristo climbed into the litter assured me I had been right. "Damn the little toadying old pederast," he muttered throwing the parcels on the cushions beside me. I hadn't expected such a violent reaction; Aristo didn't usually make such a fuss of things.

"Made a pass at you?" I asked.

"Of course he did, and you knew the old goat would. Don't even try to play otherwise. It was all I could do to refrain from punching the stuck up bastard in the mouth."

'It's not like you to react so to someone making a pass, Aristo. Did you get up on the wrong side this morning?"

"Of course not. It wasn't the pass, nor the fish eyes, nor the fluttering fingers just brushing my tunic. I know how to deal with all that as you well know. It was the insinuation -- the unbridled audacity..."

"Tell me," I instructed. As I said, it was not at all like him to be so vehement. The guy had obviously pushed Aristo too far. "Tell me."

Aristo looked over at me, deciding whether to go on.

"I want to know."

"He was pumping me, you know. About who you might be? I gave him your name and he went on digging for more until he finally came out with it."

"Out with what?"

Aristo took on an unkind imitation of the man's voice. " 'Now are you sure. I mean really sure, young man, that your master out there was never called by another name?' I asked him like what, hoping he'd catch the tone that said stop, but no... 'Oh like, Hylas maybe?' You should have seen the look on that slobbering son of a bitch. I had to beat it out here or kill him right there."

"Oh, that," I said patting his hand. I knew he was upset. "Well, I was, wasn't I? Sorry. But the past is the past and that can't be changed. I made it, I own up to it, but it does seem to drag on with these people doesn't it? You'd think I'd have been old news and long forgotten by now but that's not the way it is. And..." I took his hand firmly in mine..."We live with it, Aristo. We live with the way it is, the way it was and make what will be. Don't fret for me. I can handle it."

"They don't know you," he let the words out one at a time.

"No, they don't and never will, but they will always think they do. We can't change the stupidity of people like that. They simply are." I squeezed his arm to let him know I appreciated his protection. "Now enough of all this, let's head to Hesperia's. We'll check up on Quintus Aronius tomorrow. Let's enjoy ourselves a little." Aristo was always sensitive to what people said of my past.

Far more so than I, but by that time for me the worst part was long over, and the rehash of rumors and truth couldn't compare with actually having lived it. Let them talk. None of it could hurt me any longer. It was those around me who sometimes suffered.

Chapter 7

The trip to the Golden Wing was fortunately short. The litter, which stopped briefly at the gate, was quickly ushered into the closed courtyard which allowed its patrons to enter and exit unseen from the street. A pair of matched Persian slaves met us as we climbed out of the litter, beautiful young men with raven hair and oxen eyes who were built like stone fortresses. Definitely Hesperia's style. They were new since my last visit.

"Welcome Sirs," said one of the two, smiling while the other moved to open the heavy door.

Once inside we were met by the fluttering Calisto, the Greek majordomo from my time at the Wing.

"Numerius Meridius Pulcher," he called out, silently padding across the marble floor in soft slippers. A wide grin spread across the plump face. "How good it is to see you both. Come, come. Hesperia will be delighted. It's been too long."

"Gained a few, Calisto?" I said after he had hugged me.

"A few, yes indeed, quite a few indeed. I don't know where it comes from. I eat next to nothing but no matter how I try, I keep getting rounder. Ah, when I think of the boy I was? Ah well, time passes...You, though, stay the same. I swear by the gods. How do you do it?"

"Look closer friend. None of us stays the same."

"And Aristo – you, you are handsomer than ever. A grown man now." He looked over to me with a wink. "Matured well, didn't he? Ah well, you always had a good eye. I should be so lucky to find myself such a man."

I laughed. "Leave him be, Calisto. We all know how young you like them and as I recall longevity of affection has never been your strong point."

The cherubic eunuch laughed. "True, too true; there's just too much of a selection here at the Golden Wing. I'll notify

Hesperia immediately. Let me take you on up to her reception chamber. She's quite proud of it. It was just redone and we've got some wonderful wines. She'll be overjoyed to see you. Come. Come." We followed as he waddled before us, his bejeweled hands waving effusively as he pointed out the newest and most impressive additions since our last visit.

We waited for Hesperia in the recently remodeled reception chamber. Obviously business was good. The new decoration was as luxurious as it was lascivious, with mosaics and sculptures which portrayed the various sexual acrobatics of the gods and their mortal lovers. Apollo and Hyacinthus, Venus and Anchises, Mars and Chloe Silva complete with fluttering woodpeckers, Hercules and Hylas, Achilles and Patrocles, Aeneas and Dido, and old Jupiter and Leda, and Io, and Ganymede, and Europa. As father of the Gods I suppose he deserved the most attention.

The couches were gilded and covered in scarlet and gold satin comfy cushions. The slaves, all lookers, were well jeweled if scantily clothed. Everything was offered at the Golden Wing women and girls; boys and men, both the young and the mature. All tastes must be provided for. Any red-blooded noble Roman male would be able to find his special fantasy inside the walls of the Golden Wing. Any noble lady as well. From the most fragile virgin and the prettiest youth to the dreamt-of Amazon and longed-for gladiators; everything was available here. Hesperia had taken the offerings of the Golden Wing even further than I had done. There was a reason I had chosen her as my successor. The place might lack some of the subtlety of my managerial style but one rarely loses money underestimating the taste of Rome's wealthy. Hesperia knew what she was doing. In this business of ours, it is all about surfaces, images, fantasy. The customers are not interested in reality. We provide an escape, a very pleasant escape, but one of shallow emotion. Is it an art? I used to tell myself it was. I wanted to believe it when I was younger, wanted others to believe it. Maybe I needed to believe it. Art? I don't see it that way now; trickery at best, a moment's magical concoction for the desires of the client. But it was trickery that brought in the highest rates in the profession and the customers left happy and returned over and over again. A place like the Golden Wing doesn't survive on one time business.

"Aristo, Numerius, my darlings," Hesperia burst into the room like a clash of cymbals, hands undulating in chorus with the fine fashion of her gown. "Let me see you both. Too long, entirely too long. I am miffed with you both, leaving me in Rome so long without even a visit. Shame on you, Numerius. The country has stolen you."

"Pompeii is hardly the country," I smiled and stood to let myself be embraced in the scented warmth and enthusiasm of the woman.

"Look at you," she cried pulling back to arm's length. "Well, that sleepy little town must agree with you. I'll have to say that. Oh," her eyes caught at the jewelry. "Those are beautiful. Beautiful. Now what did you have to do for those? And I thought you had given up the trade. What have you been up to, Hylas?" Hesperia was the one person allowed to use my old name without raising rancor.

"Some of us find it simpler to just pay for our baubles rather than wait for our admirers to provide them. These days I'd be waiting a long long time and still end up with painted clay."

"Nonsense; you are the same as ever. And you Aristo, where is that boy I knew? All man now I see." Her hands fluttered lightly over his chest and biceps. "Ah, if I had only been aware of how you would turn out, I would never have let this one near you. I would have kept you all to myself. I must have been terribly shortsighted back then."

Aristo grinned at the flattery. He had always adored Hesperia. She had been the first to take the young boy under her protection at the Golden Wing and somehow managed to steer me onto the same path with the result that Aristo had been spared much of what she and I have endured. In that sense he has remained pure, a slave, perhaps, but one who has never been forced into a bed not of his own choice. That is a rare thing in Rome, especially if the slave is as attractive as Aristo. That much we were able to give him.

"You'll make him big headed, Hesperia."

Hesperia laughed. "Eh, still jealous, Hylas, after all these years? Well, come with me to my rooms, you two." She grabbed each of us by an arm and walked us out of the salon, across the atrium and toward her rooms and real office. "You know, Aristo, in our day, Hylas and I had quite a competition going as to who was the most notorious whore in Rome. As I remember, he won."

"I doubt that. Not as I remember it. Anyway it wasn't quite like that."

She laughed heartily. "Well, let's just say we gave each other a run for our money, and now look at us!"

"Enough of our scandalous history, Hesperia," I said as we entered her office. The guarded door was closed behind us. "Tell us the gossip. What is the news in Rome?" She herself sat in a chair of delicate Eastern wood while motioning us to take the cushion laden couches.

"Not good, I fear. Times are tricky right now," she said dismissing the slaves who had been placing the wine, fruit, nuts and cheeses in front of us. "There is trouble brewing in Rome."

"What kind of trouble?"

She waited until she heard the click of the door behind the exiting slaves, leaned slightly forward on the chair toward us. "Rumors, just rumors right now, but we have some fairly highly placed customers as you know…" She let the sentence wander off into thin air. "Well, we needn't say who, but the word is that Nero is making big changes, big changes."

"Such as?"

"Like, Burrus and Seneca out and Tigellinus in. He, no doubt you will remember quite well. And if that's not scary enough, it's also rumored that Claudia Octavia too is out – her place in the palace already taken over by Poppaea"

"Seneca out and Tigellinus in. That doesn't bode well at all. What is going on with our young Emperor? Seneca at least seemed to keep him somewhat in touch with reality. Now who will keep him in check? As for Poppaea, I am acquainted with that lady as she is well connected in Pompeii and what a piece of work she is. I'd steer clear of that lady, Hesperia. As far away as possible. Given power, she'll be dangerous. Tell me more of Octavia though. She was a sweet girl when her father freed me. I used to see her running about the palace before the old man had me open this place.

"No one sees her. No one hears from her. It is said she's confined to her rooms while Poppaea appears everywhere with young Nero. She must be at least 10 years older than the Emperor. He could have anyone. Why would he choose her? There's no accounting for taste."

"More like seven years, and Poppaea Sabina, like her mother before her is a great beauty, Hesperia. Two wealthy husbands already."

Hesperia laughed. "Yes, I remember Rufrius Crispinus" He visited here quite often in his day. Do you remember?"

I nodded. Poor Rufrius had fallen out with Agrippina during the reign of Claudius and been replaced by Burrus. Small wonder that when Poppaea turns up on the scene, Burrus is suddenly out of favor.

"And Otho, her current husband, at least legally. Has he ever been duped! Supposedly a good friend of Nero and now his good friend Nero steals his pretty little wife. There's divorce in the air or so it's rumored, seems Poppaea is heading for greener pastures. Some say Otho was used by the good lady just to get near the Emperor."

"With what I know of the lady in question, I have little doubt that she's been working the entire thing to her own end. Ah, but enough gossip of that family. I have lived a lifetime of their affairs, outrages and machinations. I begin to remember why I moved away to Pompeii." I leaned over the tray of fruits taking enough time with my selection to change the subject. "Do you know a Quintus Aronius, by any chance, Hesperia?"

Hesperia sat up in her chair. "Why yes. The elder or younger? The elder is stingy as Hades. The younger, well, now he's a looker and quite the ladies' man. The girls practically fight over him." She folded her hands on her lap. "Do you know the young man or just looking to know him? Is our Hylas looking to make a conquest? Well, your work will be cut out for you there, my dear. As I said, he's quite the ladies' man. At least here he shows very little interest in leaning in the opposite direction, and he is here quite frequently. I would never say never of course, you know how young men are, but Aronius seems well ensconced on my side of the street, rather like Old Claudius."

"I was fond of Old Claudius and he was very good to me, as you well know. As for Aronius, I have no designs on him, no interest in him at all really, at least not in that way. I've never even laid eyes on the lad."

"Oh, the lad is quite the charmer, Hylas. and not so much a lad as his pretty face might lead one to believe. You may change your mind and remember to keep me informed when you do. He is quite the hit when he enters our doors, I can assure you of that.

He struts around here like some foreign king followed doggishly by young Marcus Flavius. The girls adore him."

"Marcus Flavius?"

"Now, he's quite a different young fellow. That boy will try anything. He gets up to some interesting antics here, but usually not until he's followed Aronius around like a puppy for half the evening. You remember his father surely, very stuffy, even back then. Old Saddlebags. Isn't that what we use to call him?"

I nearly choked on my apricot. Of course, that was it. Old Saddlebags. I certainly hadn't recognized him. "I never would have put the two of them together and I have met the young Marcus. Didn't think much of the boy."

"Oh, he's all right," she said, taking another sip of wine. "He tries a little too hard to be daring and as I said stays glued to young Aronius while they're here, but all in all he seems a decent enough boy, young, but well meaning. A far cry better than Old Saddlebags," she said with a laugh and opened palms in the air.

"Isn't his sister a Vestal?"

Hesperia looked at me, and for a flicker of time I saw her question my motives.

"Laelia. I believe she is. Now, she is someone I know nothing about. As you can imagine the Vestal Virgins and I don't really mix."

It had been clumsy of me, asking like that, but I now knew she was lying about it. The fact that the sister of one of your customers was a Vestal would be exactly the kind of information one would know and cherish. In our business, contacts and favors from all echelons might become useful, especially such high contacts as the Vestals. Hesperia knew something and she wasn't telling. Well, we'd been friends too long for me to force it out of her, at least at this stage of the game.

She turned her attention elsewhere, changing the direction of her attention and our conversation. "Aristo, I didn't mean to ignore you for so long. How do you like Pompeii? Any thoughts of coming back to Rome for good? You could always come here with me. I am still available." Hesperia laughed and smiled at him; the door to further questions was closed. I settled back for the remainder of our visit. It lasted for the better part of an hour, and by the time Hesperia had walked us to our litter, I was more than ready to be gone.

Once in the litter and back on the street I leaned toward Aristo. "We'll have to visit young Aronius, of course. See if you can find out where he lives. Also, send a runner to see if the Vestal's slave girl has turned up. What was her name?"

"Chloe," Aristo chided. He's so much better with names, besides I know I can count on him to remember them, so why bother?

Chapter 8

Our movement toward home crept at a snail's pace. Roman traffic jams are infamous and it seemed all of Rome was out and about with the sole objective to obstruct my progress. I was frustrated, tired and gritty from just one day in Rome, the so called capital of our world. I needed a bath, a good scrape, and a soothing soak. Remembering a nearby bath from my last time in Rome, I looked over to Aristo who was busy writing on his little wax tablets that he carried everywhere. "Let's stop at Sergius' up here. I'd like to bathe before going back to the house. We have the time, I think, or nearly so anyway."

"We could send word to Metella that we're running a little tight. It's not far. The boy can be there and back in no time." said Aristo.

"Good idea, and give the fellow a little something extra since he'll be running back and forth while the rest of them are resting up." I settled back into the cushions while Aristo changed directions with the litter bearers. "Now, tell me. What did you think of our friend Hesperia?"

"She stays the same," Aristo smiled.

"I had more in mind how she answered my questions. Didn't you think she was a bit ...?"

Aristo gave me a look, kind but final. He would no more be disloyal to Hesperia than he would be disloyal to me. It was not in him. I would have to figure out her part in all of this on my own. I was sure she knew more than she admitted, but how much was she hiding and to what purpose?

The baths at Sergius' were filling up, -- great thing a Roman bath, certainly one of the great accomplishments of our culture. A Roman bath is a true delight. They're part social center, part news outlet, part spa, part business meeting, part gymnasium and pleasure house all rolled into one; marvelous things really. Time and opportunity, that's what a bath offers, time to relax, to wash off the dirt of the day and time to watch, to feel out a potential business deal, work off excess energy (or anger) in the exercise room, time to catch up on the latest news and gossip, massages that leave you invigorated or fully sated and even much more if you so desire. Everything is available at a Roman public bath. And there's something about seeing your friends and enemies nude and semi-nude that makes them quite human. A great leveler, the baths. I've always felt that if you want to get a solid take on what a man is at his core, spend an afternoon with him at the baths. Watch, listen, how does he hold himself? What does he do? Say? Where do his eyes wander? You can learn much in a bath. Does he bring a bevy of slaves or a carefully chosen one or two and bathe himself? Does he skip the exercise, or the frigidarium? Are his eyes on his friends or the slaves and which slaves exactly? Yes, much can be found out at the baths.

By the time I had exercised, sanded myself and made thorough use of Aristo and his strygil, I felt quite revived and free of grit. I was ready to enter the tepidarium for a good soak. The rather steep entry fee assured that the pool was not overcrowded. A few men lolled alone in the warm water, an older pair clinging to the side in the far corner. Sitting nude midway on the long side, two young men conversed in heavy whispers. Rather obviously, or so I thought, they displayed themselves for the admiration of the others and were quite aware of by whom and how often they were gazed at. As I entered the pool they both flexed and posed up, quite pleased with themselves. They lacked the studied air of professionals, but could probably be approached indirectly through gifts or social engagements as is the case for many a young person in Rome, who short on social standing or money or both, have only a firm young body and above average looks. I certainly had no right to disparage them. I smiled at them and moved on to the far corner. They were not unattractive lads; Rome is filled with the attractive young but they held no interest for me. Their interest in me was mildly amusing but understandable as in this situation, nude in a bath, I certainly attract my share of stares, both for the way I look and for what is missing. I have learned to live with it. It intrigues people. As a rule I wear a sheer Egyptian linen loose tunic when I bathe in public. It is a way in which I may blur certain aspects of my physique but it also attracts its own attention. Today, not having planned ahead of time, I had no option. I was nude. I ignored the stares and the interest I aroused in the preening lads who now made quite a show of jumping down into the pool in order to create a great splashing scene where they wrestled playfully with each other while keeping one eye peeled to gauge my reaction.

Scarcely had I eased myself into the corner of the large pool deciding to ignore them and to concentrate on what Hesperia wasn't telling me when I suddenly looked up to find my nephew, Quintus entering the room, good looking young man that he is, he attracted his fair share of furtive glances. Totally unaware, he looked around, spotted me and came over.

"Ah, Uncle, there you are," he said dropping his towel and slipping into the hot water and clasping my arm. "How are the baths today?"

"Well deserved, and what brings you here?" I asked noticing that the two young men who had been performing so close by had paddled off from us as Quintus approached.

"Your lad came with word of where you were and that you might be late so father sent me down to join you and let you know there was absolutely no rush as the cook had already informed him that dinner was running later than usual, something about a butcher's late delivery."

"How thoughtful of him," I said to the boy as he settled in. And how unlike Burrus. It sat wrong. Sending a quick message back with my runner was one thing, sending Quintus with this highly suspect story was another. The cook would have gone straight to Metella not Burrus.

"Have I chased off your admirers?" Quintus asked nodding his head toward the two men who had moved across the pool and stood there furtively watching us. Not waiting for an answer, he ducked his head beneath the water, rose up and with both hands, elbows spread wide, pushed the wet hair back from his face. Needless really, but an effective display. The two turned away. They would never succeed if they retreated at the first sign of competition. Quintus laughed. "I'm afraid I have."

It was time to change the subject. "I met a friend of yours today, the young Marcus Flavius. He's rather an, how shall I say it, interesting ….young man?"

Quintus colored slightly and grinned. "Well, an acquaintance actually. He's a wild one for sure. We travel in the some of the same circles."

"Yes, so I heard from the young man. The young Flavius also seems to be quite interested in my past, Quintus."

The boy bit his lip. "Like I said, he's a bit on the wild side…" He paused and evidently decided to 'fess up. "…and I'll admit that sometimes when we're a bit in the cups I may have told a few stories."

"Stories?" I arched a brow, my stern uncle act.

"I've heard a few, from Father."

"Your father? I'm surprised he would be telling them to you. It's the kind of past most respectable fathers would want to keep quiet. My past is not exactly what every Roman family hopes to be connected to."

Quintus blushed, fully this time. "Only lately. Before I turned 17 last year he was very evasive about it all. But, I had heard things, here and there, sideways comments now and then, but he refused to explain them. Then, sometime back he started telling me some of them when he was ... when we were drinking wine after dinner. Actually, I thought they were exciting; you've made something of yourself despite all you've ... what's happened to you. And, I meant no disrespect telling Marcus about them, just entertaining dinner conversation. I knew Marcus would be impressed. Sorry if I've offended."

The boy seemed sincere and to tell the truth I had much rather this response than for him to be acutely embarrassed about me. "Well, there are plenty of people who find it scandalous, Quintus. You need to be very careful, and I'm not at all sure I like the thought of being the subject of anyone's dinner conversation, but I'll forgive you and also warn you that your father may not always have his facts straight. There were so many rumors."

"He said you were the most beautiful boy in Rome."

I smiled. It was unlike Burrus to give such a compliment. "There were those who said so."

"I'm interested in knowing more", Quintus said in a confidential tone that made me momentarily uncomfortable.

"There is nothing to proud of, Quintus, except maybe for the fact that I've survived. The Fates have been kind in that respect."

"Father says you knew everyone. You were famous. Going all the way back to Old Tiberius, Caligula, Macro, Claudius and Agrippina."

Now it was my turn to blush. "All the way back indeed. Having started out as a Capri boy of Old Tiberius is nothing to be proud of." I dropped my voice after glancing around to be sure we were not being overheard. "Tiberius was an old thin shell of a man who liked to surround himself with pretty young things, male and female. I was seven and as your father's told you, a pretty young thing. There was no talent, no achievement in that, simply fact and fate. Believe me it was far from exciting. I was a slave, Quintus. It was not glamorous."

"An Imperial slave. The most famous slave in Rome ..."

"Nonsense, and famous wouldn't be the word to spring to most people's minds. Infamous perhaps but not famous."

"But Claudius freed you."

"He was a kind man."

"You knew Sejanus. Some even say..."

"Now, that is utter nonsense," I interrupted before the boy could finish the statement. "Wherever does your father get his information? Indeed your mother and I may have indeed had different fathers, but Sejanus certainly was not my father. Rumor. Vicious rumor." I tried to sound certain about it. It has been a most persistent rumor since the time of Caligula and one I had special cause to want to be unfounded.

"But you knew him."

"Yes, yes I knew him, him, and Macro and Caligula, even the old Livia. I knew the whole rotten bunch, and believe me, they were all rotten."

"Father says he knew you back then, before he'd met mother, when he was still a guard."

I didn't like the hint of innuendo in his voice. Surely Burrus had not told the boy all about that. "Enough of this, Quintus." I spoke louder than I had intended and regretted the look of chagrin that swept over the boy's features. I breathed deeply and started again. "Look Quintus, we can sit and have a nice long chat about my past if you want. You're old enough now and the gods know it will come up. I suppose you have a right to know what the gossip is all about and I will tell you what's true and what's not. But here and now is not the place. Forgive me if I've been harsh, but it isn't always easy for me to remember these things. They happened. They were real and I accept them as a part of my life, a part of what I am. I also accept my part in it all, for I made decisions all along the way. Still, many of the memories I made, or helped to make are not pleasant ones that I enjoy spreading about in the light of day. Now..." I smiled pulling myself up and moving toward the steps at the end of the pool." I think a quick dip in the frigidarium will do us both good." I climbed up out of the pool and stood for a moment letting the water run from my body wishing for my Egyptian cotton tunic while Aristo hurried across the room with my towel.

Behind me I heard Quintus follow, but I could not allow myself to turn back and look. Naturally the boy was curious, but in Jupiter's name what was Burrus stuffing the lad's head with?   I padded off to the frigIdarium followed by Aristo and Quintus, all too aware of the eyes of the room either avoiding me or unabashedly locked onto me.   The two young men in the pool grinned suggestively as I passed them and I bit my tongue to refrain from the cutting comments that flooded my mind. I was in no mood. The memories of the past had made me angry. I bristled at what I was, had been and the machinations of fate. I was hot and sorely needed the frigidarium to cool me down.

Afterward, I sent Aristo on to check on the troops and any progress at the new house. On the ride home in the litter with Quintus, we laughed. I promised to tell him more, and apologized the best I could for my earlier curtness. As for him, like any youth, he bounced back to normal with the resilience of the young. It was a pleasant ride, and we arrived back at the house in time for a quick change before a hearty meal which passed pleasantly without any of the discord of the previous day's dinner. Metella sparkled, Burrus managed to remain sober, and I retired early to my bed, alone and glad of it. Pulling the light sheet over me, I lay listening to the night sounds and going over the information we'd gained during the day.

I would have to talk with Pausina again; surely she knew something more that would be helpful. And as for Hesperia, I was certain she knew more than she was saying. It was unlike her to hold out on me, but then again I was a part of her past and she no doubt was handling quite a full present. Marcus Flavius on the other hand seemed sincere if a bit scattered and feckless. I couldn't see the boy doing in his sister for the sake of the family honor. No, the boy was sincere if rather a mess.

I made a mental list for the next day. I needed to talk to Pausina, find Quintus Aronius, and rather more than anything to locate that slave girl, Chloe. She would be able to help me find, if anyone could, the right boyfriend just in case I was wrong about Aronius. I might even want to revisit the old man Flavius. He certainly had become stuffy enough to feel the precious toes of his honor stepped on, but enough to kill his own daughter? That seemed a bit extreme for this day and age. There had been a time when that would have made sense in Rome, but even Augustus had merely exiled his own daughter, Julia. That had been over fifty years earlier, and even at the time most people had found it excessive. Of course with Laelia being a Vestal, it drove up the stakes somewhat. The ancient laws concerning a Vestal's virginity still stood. At the very least, regardless of my assessment of the old man, it was an avenue which I had to explore further. As for the old woman on the Viminal mentioned by the perfumer, I could see no reason to disturb her. But as to the slave girl who bought the perfume? Well, I would bet gold to carrots that would be our Chloe.

I fell asleep listening to the spring night and the rumble of the carts finally allowed access to the city streets. All in all it was nice to be back in Rome.

Chapter 9

I woke with a start from a dream about Tigellinus and those awful days of Caligula and, more startling, to the dim sight of a man standing over my bed, naked.

"It's all right, Uncle." It was Quintus's voice all right and I wasn't pleased.

"Venus on a stick, what are you doing?" I grabbed the bed's covers around me like a virgin threatened with imminent rape by the Gauls.

For a moment Quintus stood there motionless as my eyes adjusted to the dark. He was naked, stark. Poised to climb into my bed, he had hovered there, caught just in time.

"Oh shit," he said as he crumpled to a seat on the end of my bed, elbows on his knees and hands in his head. "Shit, shit, shit."

I gathered the sheet around me and jumped from the bed as if it were on fire. "What is going on here, Quintus? This is ridiculous."

He looked up at me tears of frustration gathering about the corners of his eyes. "It is ridiculous, I know it. I should have realized. I should never have listened to him. I should have known he was wrong about this."

"Who? About what? What are you talking about, Quintus" I sat down in a chair still wrapped in my sheet, calmer now but not happy. "And put something on, boy. This is way off the beam, Quintus. Cover yourself and tell me what all this is about. I want the truth. You've been acting quite odd ever since the first night of my arrival. Give it up Quintus. Out with it. I'm your Uncle, by Jupiter, and regardless of what you've heard about me - from your father or anyone else- I do have some scruples. What's all this about anyway? If what you want is male, there's plenty about more your own age who would be happy to oblige any young man who looks as you do. Besides, unless I'm very wrong your predilections lay much more in the other direction.   So what's going on? Time to 'fess up. It's becoming an embarrassment for both of us. Between you and your friend Marcus I've had quite enough. At least his interest is sincere if blatantly pursing the hedonistic. Yours on the other hand is manufactured. What's the story? Out with it now."

Quintus sat hunched on the bed listening to my tirade then he began to laugh. "Venus on a stick, indeed." he gasped between the spurts of laughter. "By the god's…" he flopped onto his back still laughing. "What a stupid idea. I should have known. I should have…"

"Known what?"

He wiped his eyes and sat up, propped on one elbow, now completely at ease. "That father was wrong. Wrong about you, wrong about what I should do; just wrong across the board." He laughed again and stood moving unselfconsciously to the chair opposite me. "And you're right, although I won't deny having known a few boys here and there, given the choice I'll choose the woman every time. Jupiter, I'm sorry. It was a crazy idea, Uncle."

"So tell me about it," I said more relaxed now. "If you can stop laughing long enough. I think I deserve the full explanation. Pull yourself together and out with it." I managed a smile and released the death grip on my covers. "Tell me."

Quintus rubbed his eyes and nodded. "Yes, okay. Yes, give me just a moment. I'm ready to confess all."

He finally pulled himself together, took a deep breath and began to run through it. "Father had this crazy idea, what with your building the new house and coming back to Rome, where, as he says, there are countless men ready to do anything to get hold of your fortune ... that you could well afford your choice of young men. Well, he thought that it would be better for the family if that choice were one of us. You get the picture?" He ended, a bit nervous but looking me straight in the eye, and I approved of that.

"I get the picture." This was a new low even for Burrus. "So he ...advised ... you to ..." I started to say seduce me but the word seemed laughable when applied to me. "Offer yourself?"

Quintus smiled and nodded. "He said I wouldn't be the first of the family ..."

"Stop there. Your father's a real jewel, Quintus. Whatever was he thinking? And as for the other bit; he told you about that? What did he tell you exactly?"

"Only that he had played Hercules to your Hylas."

It was my turn to color. "Well, for his information I have no intention of playing Claudius to your Agrippina. Did he really say Hercules? I'm afraid your father overrates himself. I hope he also informed you that whatever may or may not have happened, it was long before he met you mother. I hope he told you that."

Quintus nodded fighting for control but looking as if he were about to burst into another fit of laughter.

"Did he happen to mention that at the time I had no choice in the matter?"

"Do you think Father would? Still it wasn't hard to figure out the time line." He was bubbling with laughter again. "You should have been there, seen it, while he explained rather obliquely what was to be permitted and what was not."

"Your father's very Roman about these things."

"I know he was wrong. I know I shouldn't have listened to him, that the whole thing was rather stupid on both our parts, but he really thought it would be best for the family."

"Venus on a stick, the man can still infuriate me with his ignorance. But yes I can see where he might believe it. It would fit his twisted logic. I trust your mother knows nothing about all this?"

"Of course not. Not a thing. Father warned me against it."

"Well at least that's something in his favor."

"Don't be angry with us, Uncle. I know he can be a real clod sometimes, but you know him and how he is; and as for me," he smiled charmingly, "well, you know you've always been my favorite Uncle."

"I'm your only Uncle, you impertinent snip," I couldn't keep my scowl from breaking into a smile. The boy had charm.

Quintus grinned and offered me his hand. "So, we're forgiven?"

"You are," I answered grasping his hand, "And I suppose even your father will have to be forgiven. After all, he is who he is."

Quintus smiled again. It was quite a winning smile.

"And I want you to reassure your father for me that the new house on the Quirinal will eventually go to your sister, Lucia. I don't want the two of you fighting over this one and a woman should have some security, the same as a man. You can assure him that you both will be provided for."

"That should suffice for him, and let us both off the hook." Quintus crossed the room and picked up the short tunic he had dropped on the floor at the foot of my bed. He would make some young lady very happy. "And just what would you have done, if I had responded to your advances?"

Quintus cinched the belt tightly around his narrow waist. "Hmm. I would have crossed that Rubicon when I came to it. After all, you're still very attractive ... for a person of your age."

I threw a cushion from the chair at his head which he caught and threw back at me.

"Now get back to your own bed and let an old man get some sleep. Lucky for you you're such a charmer and I'm such an understanding Uncle. Now get out."

Quintus winked. "Goodnight then. You probably do need that beauty sleep. I on the other hand- well, it's still far too early for me to go to my own bed. But don't worry, I have other options."

"I just bet you do. But go for Jupiter's sake. Go bother someone else."

"As you wish." He left the room with a flourish and a bounce in his step I had not seen since my arrival. It was a good to see. As for me, I stumbled back to bed and slept the sleep of the dead.

Chapter 10

I breakfasted with the family. We were sitting in the garden near a gardenia bush which was sending forth a ravishing scent. Aristo had shown up at the crack of dawn with my morning drink and to get me prepared for our busy day. I felt good. Awake, ready and free of the angst of the last few days with Quintus and Burrus.   The olives I had carried along for the house from Pompeii were especially good and Metella had some excellent preserved figs to slather on the fresh bread.

"Anyone familiar with the Quintus Aronius family?" I asked between bites. "Live up on the Janiculum."

"I knew a Marcus Aronius, years ago, in the guard, but he was not from here. Came from Puetulli, I think." Burrus said nursing his cup of watered wine. "Good soldier, old Marcus…"

"Too early for war stories, dear," Metella said laying a hand on his. "Eat your breakfast." She looked tired, blue circles beneath her eyes not fully hidden by her cosmetics. She seemed to be wearing more these days than I remembered. It was unlike her. She had always used her brushes sparingly and try as I might, I had never succeeded in interesting her in my expensive taste for the more exotic cosmetics from the far corners of the empire.

"I do." said Quintus, swallowing his bread and figs without looking up. He seemed to have quite an appetite. "At least I know the son. He's a good friend of Marcus Flavius. We've been to some dinner parties together. Don't know much about the family though. Except his father's some bigwig in the finance corps. At least that's the way Marcus tells it."

"Friends with Marcus Flavius?" I selected a few more olives. It made perfect sense. Aronius moved to position number one.

"And what exactly is your interest in the Aronii, Numerius?" Metella asked looking slyly at me from across the table.

"Are you on one of your hunts, one of your so called games? I'd have thought you'd given those up at your age. I thought that's why you retired to Pompeii."

I shrugged my shoulders. "Just a little something for a friend."

"And what friend would that be, Numerius?"

"A nameless friend."

"Nameless friends are never a good sign. I do hope you'll be careful. We've grown used to a certain amount of peace and quiet in this house. I shouldn't want to stir up things too much."

"I'll do my best." I smiled back at her. "Nothing dangerous as far as I know." Well that was true thus far, wasn't it? At least it hadn't been dangerous for me, as of yet.

"Hmm." She was unconvinced.

"Can I help?" asked Quintus asked all smiles.

"Certainly not," said Metella.

"Why not, Metella? Might do the boy good to spend some time with his uncle. You're always saying the boy has too much free time on his hands. This will give him something to do and he could learn a lot from Numerius," said Burrus eagerly. I could see the wheels turning in his head and assumed Quintus had not yet spoken to him about the events of last night. Metella looked at her husband in surprise but said nothing.

"Can I, Uncle?" Quintus beamed at me across the table. "You used to promise that when I was older. Well, now I am. Wouldn't it be nice to spend time together?" He was grinning like a maniac. "I think Father's right, we should spend more time together." He looked at his father who nodded in agreement. The boy was having him on and I couldn't honestly say I disapproved.

"Well, we'll see how it goes. There is one thing you might help me with. I'd like to meet this young Aronius without having to approach him directly. Maybe you could host a little party. That I will gladly pay for," I added quickly seeing Metella's face tighten. "I'm sure you know some place suitable. Somewhere your young friends will feel relaxed. Let's say Aronius, Marcus Flavius and four or five others, preferably friends of theirs. Can you put that together?"

"Easily done. I know just the place."

"Get whatever front money you need from Aristo. I have another meeting this morning that I have to make alone."

"Done," said Burrus banging his hand on the table, pleased as punch with himself.

"Done," smiled Quintus right back at him.

I ignored the wink of Burrus to his son and excused myself from the table to prepare for my trip to the House of the Vestals.

I entered without fanfare through a side gate as agreed on for my meeting with Pausina. She received me in a small enclosed pavilion off the garden, which she ordered carefully closed up before we began.

"I have a few questions." I decided the direct approach would be best.

"Ask away, Numerius. I'll answer as I can." Pausina seemed calm this morning, confident and far different than the lady of my last visit. Perhaps she thought it was all under control.

"About Marcus Flavius, just how often did he visit his sister here?"

"Yes, "she raised a graceful hand to wave in dismissal. "You're right. More than probably was wise of me. And I was aware that she slipped out at night to meet him. Yes, I knew that too. But, I was fond of the girl, but then I know the restrictions of this place all too well. Still, yes, I was probably too lax with her."

"And you knew this how?"

"Through the slave girl, Chloe. She was devoted to Laelia of course, but she also knew better than to cross me. Chloe is a smart girl. She knew where her first loyalties should lie. If she had known who Laelia was seeing, I'm sure I would have known that as well."

"Have you heard from her yet?"

Pausina sighed spreading her hands. "Ah, Numerius, the poor thing is probably terrified and frankly, under the circumstances, she probably is getting as far away from Rome as her looks and whatever spending money she's accumulated can get her. I shouldn't think a girl like Chloe would have such a difficult time of it. My guess is she's a far piece down the road toward a new life by now."

That seemed a bit casual to me. I noted it but said nothing. "I did find the perfumer and we're looking into the buyers. One was a slave girl, I assume that would be our missing Chloe.

"And the others, who are they?"

"Still working on them." I don't like to bring up names until I've checked them out. Sometimes you speak too quickly too freely as to where you're headed and live to regret it. There are persons to share the bits and pieces with (mine would be Aristo) and you do well to keep it all from the others until you're sure.

"The news of Laelia's death will be released officially today, Numerius. It appears we've avoided any gossip. We may be able to move on without interruption." Pausina didn't look at me directly, rather at something over my right shoulder that I knew wasn't there. It's surprising what you can tell by where someone is looking when they speak to you.

"Are you wanting me to stop my investigation?"

"Oh, no, certainly not. I want to know who the man was, for one thing. I just want us to go about it carefully. Especially now that it appears we've gotten through the part of Laelia's death without rumor. I don't want our actions to make others too curious. If you understand what I mean."

"I understand." And I did understand. She wanted me to back off. What I didn't understand, what she wasn't telling me, was why? Quite an about face from two nights earlier. "What about the other slaves? It might help if I could talk to some of them. The girl Chloe must have had a close friend or two."

Pausina bit her lip. "I'd prefer not, Numerius. I doubt they know anything and as I said I'd rather not stir up anything else. Not yet anyway. Can't we avoid it for the time being? All seems to be quiet on that front. I'd like to keep it that way. Can't we wait until it's absolutely necessary?"

"Of course we can," I responded perhaps a bit tightly. What choice did I have? She wasn't letting me anywhere near them. First Hesperia and now Pausina. I didn't like it when my friends started holding back. It ticked me off, especially with Pausina who had involved me in the first place.

"Ah, Numerius don't be angry with me. We just can't deal with a scandal right now. Please understand. I was caught unawares the other night. I may have over-reacted. It does seem we have it under control now and I think maybe we'd be wiser to just move on. Surely, you can understand my position?"

I smiled, it wasn't easy for me, but I smiled. "Of course I understand." Like hell I did, but I would before it was all over. "I'm sorry if I was being dense."

"Not at all, Numerius, but the danger is past, and I think it best we put it all to sleep. Sometimes getting to the bottom of things stirs up more dust than it's worth. We've accomplished what we needed. There's been no hint of scandal. I'd like to keep it that way. Let's stop while we're ahead."

"I see your point." She did have a point, but I didn't like it a bit. "So, it's over?" I stood, ready to go.

"Oh, don't look so glum; don't pout Numerius." Pausina laughed rising and coming close enough toward me to lay a hand on my arm. "Forgive me for being a silly overwrought woman, for old times' sake? We have quite a past, Numerius. This wouldn't be the first secret we've kept, now would it?"

It was only polite to laugh back.

"And some were far more dangerous to us than this. Still friends?"

"Of course we are."

"Good." She linked arms with me steering me toward the door all smiles and gushing girl now, and almost convincingly.

"Ah, we were a pair, weren't we Numerius? Two scared kids playing our dangerous little games. We've survived them and done rather well for ourselves, don't you think?"

I couldn't help but think that there was a warning in there, no matter how gently put forth. We said our goodbyes and I slipped out the way I had come.

I was back at the house in the Palatine by mid-morning. Disgruntled by my interview I sat in the garden sipping on a fruit juice concoction Metella currently favored. Aristo was off overseeing the work on the house. Quintus was out; no doubt arranging his dinner party unaware that now there would be no need. Well, let him do it, I decided suddenly angry. There's always a good enough reason for a dinner party when you're his age and I still would like to see this Aronius lad. Why not have the dinner and if I found out something, for my own enlightenment of course, what could it matter to anyone? I don't like loose ends. If Pausina was satisfied then that was her. As long as I avoided kicking up any dust, who'd be any the wiser?

"Will we disturb you if we work in the garden?" Andronicus asked approaching my chair and followed by the imposing Apollo stripped to the waist for work and carrying the plants which we had brought from Pompeii. "I would like to get these in the ground as soon as possible."

"Not at all, Andronicus, not at all. Go right ahead, by all means. Where are they going?"

"Over there by the lilies. The sun should be just right there, I think."

"Yes, yes, you're probably right, not too much water though. They like it dry. And, make the hole wide, well…" I stopped in response to the slave's raised eyebrow. "Listen to me telling you," I waved my hand. "Go to, Andronicus. Have at it."

For the next better part of an hour I watched the two dig, fertilize, plant and water their new prized ward. Or rather, I watched Apollo work under the constant eye and direction of Andronicus. There are worse ways to amuse oneself than watching someone of Apollo's looks labor in the warm sun. It always amazes me how some men look so good in sweat, something I avoided if at all possible. On Apollo it looked good. Very good indeed.

"Stop eyeing the help, Uncle." Quintus said suddenly appearing over me. I hadn't noticed the boy enter. He was beaming, obviously proud of himself. "It's all set. Tonight. Aronius, Marcus Flavius and three others whom we all know. I'll tell you about them later.   Marcus, though, well I'm afraid I had to entice him a bit by telling him you'd be present and hinting more than a bit that you might well be amenable to sharing some of your stories. He wasn't about to turn that down." Quintus grinned. "You'll have to give the poor bugger something, Uncle. I promised."

"As long as it's limited to stories, I can oblige and I assume stories are all you promised?"

"All I promised for certain anyway. Now, what I might have hinted at … well, I'll leave that to your imagination." He grinned again.

"The gods forbid, Quintus. I probably don't want to know. Don't tell me. We're in a bit of a knot though. For reasons known only to herself, Pausina wants me out of it."

"No," the boy looked crestfallen.

"I said she wants me out, not that I was giving it up. I don't like being turned away, especially when I was invited in the first place. We'll be discreet of course, but I for one want to know more and some of it I intend to find out at dinner tonight." I took the bulla I had been holding in my hand and gave it to the boy. "Now, here's what I want you to do."

He sat eagerly and for the next bit of time we went over my plans for the evening. By the time we had finished and he had gone to ready things Andronicus and Apollo had also finished their labors. With no further reason to linger in the garden I decided on a quick nap before preparations for the evening.

Chapter 11

Aristo and I left for the dinner by rented litter and accompanied by the specially chosen bearers costumed to make a particular statement, one that had little to do with taste. Appearance is everything in Rome and tonight I was putting on a show for the young friends of Quintus. The young gardener Apollo was with me to serve as the window dressing the young   Marcus Flavius would expect of me. Apollo had readily agreed to it. Happy to get out and about, he was not the least self-conscious about his own skimpy costume, or more to the point, the lack of it. We moved at a good clip down the Palatine, across the forum and into the Subura where the dinner was to be held. Quintus, as host, had gone on before us. It was early and the Subura streets were busy if not full of merry makers out for the evening. Out as usual were the regular Subura thieves, whores, and the general masses looking for some evening entertainment. The establishment Quintus had picked was not in the safest of neighborhoods but certainly one their youth would find interesting for carousing.

The establishment Quintus had picked for his dinner, The Rollicking Pig, was not far up the main street leading into the Subura and that seemed a good thing as that area tends to be pretty rough after dark. We were greeted outside the door by two burly slaves who looked like ex-gladiators. By the looks of them our litter would be safe from any passersby, at least any the two hulking slaves weren't in cahoots with.

Once inside the heavy door we were ushered across a somewhat rustic atrium past what was obviously the common room already filled with what appeared to be a mix of Rome's best and brightest young men and an assortment of shady characters providing them the opportunity to rub elbows with persons their families would have been scandalized by. Certain young men love walking on the wild side and this was obviously the place to mix with the seamier inhabitants of Rome's population on a rather "safer" footing judging by the conspicuous display of more muscle bound slaves like those at the door posted around the perimeter of the room and carefully monitoring the proceedings.

We were ushered to a private banquet room toward the back of the establishment which must have taken up a good part of the ground floor of the insula. It was decorated with murals of satyrs and nymphs in which the artist had made up for with excessive gusto for his subject, what he had lacked in technique. On the far wall spread a colorful Rape of Lucretia with a Sextus of rather mythic proportions; Jupiter doing the dirty deed with a somewhat surprised looking Ganymede presided on the second ; and on the third wall Venus and Mars were about to engage. Something for everyone.

"Gentlemen, our guest of honor has arrived," Quintus stood and announced. "Numerius Meridius Pulcher, also known as Hylas." There was a moment of quiet while all eyes turned toward us. We had arranged this ahead of time and I had dressed carefully to dazzle with enough jewels to be either an empress or a very high priced whore with no taste. With that, combined with Aristo in carefully exposed finery and Apollo in his near nakedness by my side, I expected that we lived up to the preconceived notions of even Marcus Flavius. It never hurts to give people something to gawk at when you'd prefer them not to see what it is you are really doing.

"Come, Uncle.   We have saved you the place of honor."

As I settled onto my couch and Aristo exchanged my sandals for dinner slippers, Quintus introduced me to the young men present. They were already in the first flush of the effects of a more than respectable imitation Falerian wine with which the rented slave boy of Quintus moved continually about topping up the oversized cups. Drunkenness was part of the plan. The slave boy was young and attractive and I easily spotted the chain on which the bulla was hung disappearing beneath the boy's light and filmy tunic. He was a stunner and I figured we'd paid well for him, an expensive trinket, but I could afford it and the boy certainly set a tone. Details matter.

"We've already met," Marcus Flavius grinned raising his cup. "I have been looking forward to this evening ..." he paused and I suspected he was unsure of whether or not to call me by my old name. "It isn't often that we dine with someone so famous."

"Infamous, I think you mean, young Flavius." I smiled even allowing myself a small wink in his direction to establish his perceived position of already being a familiar, a fact he was no doubt proud of, giving him one or two steps up on the worldliness scale as these youngsters saw things.

I was then introduced to the others. They were a fairly innocuous group of young men from good families playing at depravity and wildness but far more pedestrian than they would have hoped. Aronius would have been easy to pick out even without the introductions, a real stunner of a Roman youth. Twenty or more, he was hard bodied but with that golden boy aura of the finest patrician homes. His smile was dazzling, one that caught you in the gut and for a moment I tried to remember where I'd seen it before. It wasn't there, too many smiles over the years. To wait on him, he had brought along a truly striking young Egyptian girl in a fantastic red wig. Whether she belonged to him or was rented like some of our entourage was hard to tell.

Marcus Flavius had brought quite a looker himself. The boy, probably Syrian, was no more than sixteen and was dressed almost as scantily as Apollo to an entirely different effect. The two together could have easily posed for the Jupiter/Ganymede mural. The other young men were accompanied by what appeared to be their personal body slaves and were for the most part pleasing enough but unspectacular.

Quintus signaled for the first course, of shellfish and eggs prepared in a dozen inventive ways which was brought in by a bevy of lovely young girls dressed to tease. The banquet was on. As the dinner progressed, each course brought in alternately by a team of girls or boys, each team more seductively adorned than the previous one,the conversation moved from generalities to more and more colorfully detailed stories of personal escapades. All the while Quintus' little slave assiduously made the rounds with his wine pitcher. The thing was costing me a bundle no doubt, but what was my money for? By the time we reached the honeyed cakes, fruit and cheese, everyone was well on their way to the next morning's hangover and the servers were nearly nude except for strategically placed bangles. I watched the young men drinking happily, joking, taking liberties with the servers, appreciating this or that one as their tastes dictated. Aronius was like a demigod, sure of himself and his golden place in humanity. Marcus Flavius spent a good amount of his time gazing at that young man, a curious mix of admiration and lust which Aronius ignored completely. Still, I could see a connection there whatever the details.

"Come sit with me. You are too far away, young Marcus. Here." I patted the cushions of my couch and smiled at the young man, a signal previously arranged with Quintus. It is always a good idea when you want to see something unobserved to provide a totally different thing for all the others to watch.

The young Flavius nearly bounded across the couches to join me. "Ah, yes, time to get comfortable, gentleman," Quintus announced and turned to his slave boy with the wine. "Now, Giton, and fill up the wines." He winked at the boy who at once dropped his tunic to the floor. As previously agreed Apollo followed suit.

Marcus Flavius laughed and ordered his boy to do the same. The others soon followed suit, slaves and masters alike stood or reclined in their natural state plus or minus a few jewels or trinkets.

While I drew all eyes to my outrageous flirtation and appreciation of Marcus Flavius' body, I kept my real attention on the slave <u>Giton </u>who, as instructed, made the rounds with his wine pitcher, the golden bulla now exposed against his naked skin. Flavius hardly noticed the boy, nor did the others bar one, who was definitely not interested in the bulla given the way his hand wandered. Then the boy reached Aronius. I saw the eyes stop, focus and then look up at the boy's face. He said nothing but the brain went into gear. He glanced at the rest of us all seemingly focused on my dalliance with Marcus Flavius, and to cover he pulled his young Egyptian beauty onto his couch.

"Well," I said pulling myself slightly away from young Flavius now that I had accomplished my goal. "I promised, or rather I believe my nephew promised, young Marcus here a story or two. So what is it you'd like to know about, gentlemen? I will share what I can." Several topics came up immediately. Tiberius and Capri, Caligula, the Golden Wing and my personally most hated, Sejanus.

Skirting the last of these I launched into various anecdotes pleasing enough to their interest in the salacious but basically harmless.

The rest of the evening, wine still pouring, slid rapidly and steadily down the hillside from decency to debauchery, or at least their youthful version of it. Still to my experienced and jaded eye it was distasteful, for in their youthful excesses their futures peeked out unknown to them. By the time Aristo, Apollo and I were ready to make our departure, I had seen more than enough. Young men playing at depravity often found their way into the real thing sooner than they would think. Boys like Quintus might escape with occasional flirtations, but Marcus Flavius was already well on his way and with Aronius probably a step ahead already. Where would they be as fully grown men? I didn't want to think of it.

Pleading my age, I took leave of the young men much to the chagrin of Marcus Flavius who had every right to expect that he was to have received much more than just my stories. It was time to go. We said goodnight to all and left them to play amongst themselves.

Once safely inside the litter and headed down to the forum I turned to Aristo, eager to talk over my ideas. "Young Aronius, "I said pointing a finger at him. "He's the lover or I'm a Vestal myself. He recognized the bulla instantly and wondered where the boy had got it. That much was obvious."

"Or he knew the bulla and had no idea where it had gone to," Aristo added calmly, always the one to pull me back from my mental leaps.

"First the perfume then the bullla? No, no. Definitely the lover and probably the murderer. An easy case don't you think?"

"Perfume plus bulla does not necessarily equal lover and killer. I'll give you the lover."

"That's generous of you, Aristo. So you'll go for lover but not for the killer, eh?"

" Lover indeed. As for the other, let's wait and see. It's a little too neat for my tastes." Aristo was being moody and I suspected I knew why. "And what about Marcus Flavius?" he asked. "Now there's a piece of work. If he's in mourning for his sister you certainly couldn't tell it by his actions tonight."

"You're too harsh on him, Aristo. Granted he has his flaws but remember some find forgetfulness, even if momentarily, in hard drinking and play. He'd not be the first to drown his grief in wine and lust. Not uncommon when you think of it."

"The boy is a degenerate," Aristo flatly stated leaving little room for his opinion of the boy. "And the way you were fawning over him ..."

"It was for a purpose. I wasn't ..."

"You seemed to be having quite a time of it."

"Oh, no you don't," I injected hoping to steer clear of the hole I was about to fall in. Aristo rarely got his back up about such things, but when he did, well; he could make my life miserable without ever stepping outside the bounds of propriety. "He's just a lad. I was acting."

"He wasn't. You haven't seen the last of young Marcus Flavius. Mark my words."

"Oh rest assured. I can handle Marcus Flavius. No need to worry there."

"So you say." he smiled, a small concession, but it meant he would come around and I'd be allowed off the hook.

Aristo grinned. "At least we've finally seen proof of the boy's relation to Old Saddlebags."

I laughed loudly. "Yes, obviously the apples don't fall very far from the ..." The litter lurched to a sudden stop interrupting my carefully phrased quip.

"Bastard," I heard a strange voice bark and the sound of an ensuing scuffle. Before Aristo and I could jump out of the litter, it was over. We were surrounded by eight men, clubs, daggers and gladii – no contest. We were dead meat if they were so inclined. Apollo lay crumpled at the feet of one of the apes who brandished a club, but by the looks of it he had taken down two of the fellows before he'd gotten knocked out of it. The litter bearers stood frozen. They had nothing to gain by playing brave and they knew it.

"Get them up," one of the better equipped apes spoke to the others while pointing his gladius in my direction. They looked like body guards rather than a gang. It suddenly occurred to me that this wasn't a robbery or random violence. It was official business.

"You, Numerius Meridius Pulcher, whatever you are, you need to keep your nose out of other people's business. Do you understand?"

"I think I get the point." I said calmly. "But, I don't suppose you'd want to tell me for whom you are delivering the message?"

The ape laughed, or at least snorted in what could be taken for a laugh. "Right, nice try, Meridius, but no deal. Just butt out, because the next time we have to be sent after you, we'll do more than bust up your pretty slave toy. You got it?"

"Seems crystalline clear." I responded before Aristo's hand on my arm told me to stop. "I got it."

"Good," he grunted, unaware of my mocking him. "Okay boys – sling those other two over a shoulder and we're done here." He snorted again. "Taken down by a fancy bed boy. That'll teach 'em." He turned back to me as the others gathered up their two fallen comrades. "Go, and remember what I said, Numerius

Meridius Pulcher," he stressed the cognomen in full blown disdain. "Go home, and take yourself and your pretty boys back home to Pompeii before you end up with more than you bargained for. Next time I'll set my boys free on you. And believe me it won't all be fun. Cinaedus," he spat the vulgar slur and turned back to his men. "Let's go lads," he barked at the men and they were gone as quickly as they had appeared.

We managed to get Apollo up and onto the litter, a nasty lump on the back of his head. It looked like he'd survive but he'd certainly have a hell of a hangover in the morning that wasn't from the wine at the dinner party.

"Head for home," I ordered the litter bearers while Aristo and I walked silently beside it. "It's all okay now, and there will be extra gratuities for all concerned." We trudged on toward the forum and home without speaking. I wasn't ready to talk now, too many feelings, thoughts and directions. I had to think. Funny how such an encounter can clear the haze of even the best wine.

Chapter 12

Back on the Palatine, Andronicus opened the door for us and we put Apollo, hurting but conscious, to bed with compresses and a warm herbal drink that Aristo swore by. Luckily for us all and to our great relief, Quintus arrived home shortly thereafter, unassailed. Thank the gods Quintus had not been with us. Metella would not be happy as it were. My sister's motherly wrath would have been far worse to face than that swearing ape and his men. I counted us lucky on that one.

Quintus, Aristo and I sat in my rooms as dawn approached. The attack and warning put an entirely different spin on my figuring. Aronius obviously had had no time to plan and send the men to intercept us.

"Perhaps not so simple as I had first thought." I smiled weakly at Aristo.

"Hmm," Aristo's mono-syllabic answer was enough. He was never one to say I told you so. He stood over me kneading the knots out of my shoulder. He was always thoughtful that way; like any truly superior slave he knew what I needed before I did and quietly set to it.

"You're not going back to Pompeii, are you?" Quintus asked eagerly. "I mean we're not giving up that easily, are we?"

"We are not. No. But the 'we' here means Aristo and me. Under the circumstances I think your mother would prefer your quick exit from this particular project."

"Not a chance," Quintus exclaimed. "Besides, father has already given his blessing to it."

"Your father may find his mind changed when your mother gets hold of him. I've known my sister for a long time. I've seen her in action."

"Oh, no doubt he'll pay a price. But mother won't contradict him openly. You should know that about her by now. He is the paterfamilias after all. She won't be happy about it, but she won't take back what was said."

"Maybe you could suggest your own withdrawal?" I offered without much hope. I really didn't want Metella upset, especially not with me, and there was the safety of Quintus to worry about.

"Not on your life, no way. It's just getting interesting," Quintus said folding his arms across his chest. "You're stuck with me, Uncle, like it or not."

"Knowing your mother, if anything happens to you it may well be my life." Obviously the lad was not going to give that much, flushed with excitement and all eagerness, no. I knew the symptoms myself. Quintus was hooked. I didn't relish the talk I knew would be forthcoming with Metella, but in the words of old Caesar, the die was cast and we would all have to live with it. "But it's not all decadent parties like tonight, you know."

Quintus grinned, recognizing victory when it happened. "Of course," he nodded. "But that wasn't all too bad in itself, was it? The bulla thing worked didn't it? You were right about that."

"Maybe, maybe not, Aronius certainly recognized it, but our little run in tonight puts a different light on things." I signaled to Aristo that I'd had enough and he went off to find my bedtime drink.

"How so, exactly?" Quintus asked.

I sat back and sighed.   "Even if these were hired thugs, and I don't think they were, they would have had to been arranged for. I doubt any of our dinner guests would have had those connections. I could be wrong, but it's not likely, and since in all probability they weren't hired – they had all the ear markings of body guards – that means we're dealing with a different kettle of fish. It had to be someone rich and powerful enough to have such a group and to know how to use them, someone who obviously wants the matter closed.

"Lots of people have bodyguards these days."

"You mean lots of people have one or two perhaps but not eight or more that all look like ex-gladiators. No, this is someone above the regular ilk of Roman comfort. Trust me on that."

"Then, who?"

"Pausina perhaps," the name slipped out before I had time to stop it. "But I don't think so. It doesn't feel right. Besides, I'm fairly certain I gave her the impression that I had agreed to give up the investigation.   Of course it's possible that she was just underscoring her message, but I doubt it. No, not Pausina. What do you know of Aronius' father?"

"Not a lot. He's well to do judging by the money his son throws around and if Quintus Aronius isn't just bragging to increase his standing, he's a man on his way up. Or so Quintus says, very well connected.

"Connected? How so?"

"That he doesn't say, but his hints are meant to lead one to think quite highly connected."

"Imperial high?" I arched an eyebrow. I hadn't thought of that. Something definitely bugged me about the boy even if I couldn't quite put my finger on it. I definitely needed to talk to the boy himself.

Quintus threw up a hand to cover a yawn. "Who knows with him, Uncle? He's always hinting at things. I doubt half of them are true. Marcus might know more. They're the closest to each other and from the stories they tell, well they have adventures outside our group – on their own.

"Marcus and Quintus Aronius?   Now that's interesting, tell me more."

"Like I said not a lot to tell really. Just hints to whet our appetites. Women mostly, parties of the sort the rest of us are not invited to. Aronius is quite the ladies' man. That I've witnessed myself on several occasions and if Marcus is to be believed, and I have no reason not to, the womanizing I've been witnessed to is a drop in the bucket compared to what actually goes on." He stopped and yawned again.

Aristo entered, came into the room with my cup handing it to me with a glower that clearly read that it was time for sleep.

"Okay, enough of all this." It was time to stop, eat, rest, sleep or whatever the case might be. This morning it was sleep. "We all need a bit of sleep. When I wake I shall call on young Aronius and then maybe again on Marcus. Quintus, off to bed with you now. We'll talk again later. I may have something for you to do this afternoon."

Quintus stood slightly bleary eyed. "I could use a little sleep."

"You're not alone in that," I said giving his shoulder a pat. "Get some rest."

He took his leave and was no more out the door than Aristo turning down my bed and said "Drink that and get in bed. You need your sleep." And that's what I did.

In a few short hours I was up again. The hangover from the imitation Falerian wasn't too bad and by the time I'd drunk Aristo's cure and gone through the customary process of dressing I felt completely revived and ready for the day. Poor Quintus was not as lucky. When I found him in the garden, he was sitting looking at a plate of fruit and cheese and looking decidedly on the greenish side. Metella sat opposite, grim and silent.

"Morning all," I said giving her a kiss on the forehead and sitting down in a chair next to her.

"If you call this morning," Metella said quietly with a smile with all the warmth of a mountain spring in January.

"Ah," I stalled for time. I knew it was better to face the music directly, with Metella it is better to get it over with and move on. She wasn't one to let it slide and forget. "We were out a bit late. I probably should apologize for that. Totally my fault, I'm afraid."

"Yes, dawn is rather late, Numerius. I am not used to having my son return to his home as the birds are waking and certainly not in his condition. I know Burrus has approved Quintus's working with you, but I expected you to have a better influence on the boy. And poor Apollo has returned in rather worse wear than Quintus. Just look at the boy."

He did look quite off-color. I nodded. "Yes, yes. I agree totally with you, but in his defense the wine was part of the plan..."

"Of course it was, as no doubt were the dancing girls and the flute boys and Juno knows what else that went on. I would have expected this from Burrus but you, Numerius, you should know better. Just look at him."

I was looking at him and he looked as though he was about to puke; bad timing. "Yes, yes, Metella, I admit it. I was lax in my attention and will do better in the future. My apologies, dear sister, but first things first I think." I turned back to Quintus. "Aristo is in the kitchen putting my breakfast together – when he brings it in, I'll have him prepare for you a marvelous concoction he has that will completely take care of everything."

Quintus stifled a heave then stood. "I'd think I better catch him there," he said charging for the doorway. "Excuse me."

We watched him head into the house and once he was gone Metella turned to me.

"Numerius Meridius Pulcher..." The use of the full name, a sure sign of displeasure, I knew it was better to say nothing.

"I know my husband has given his approval to this nonsense," Metella began softly belying the rock hard seriousness beneath the voice, "but let me just say this and say it just once. "If anything and I mean anything happens to my son, I will hold you directly responsible. You may do as you like. You're a grown man and should know better but that's your business. I know you've lived your life around all these intrigues and others perhaps much worse, but my son has not."

"I'm quite serious. Take care with my son for all our sakes. Do you understand me? I may have to acknowledge my husband's wishes here, but it doesn't mean I have to like it. Let something happen to Quintus and I will have your manly parts and feed them to our dogs, both yours and my husband's."

I was tempted to make some comment about mine not being worth all that much, but I knew better than to try humor, so I just bit my tongue and nodded.

"Now there, it's over. Enough said. Let's have our breakfast." She picked up a roll and began spreading it with honey. "At the moment I'm prepared to go back to being a dutiful sister and wife. But just remember what I have said."

"I'll remember." I could only imagine that Burrus had gotten much the same speech. I wondered how he had taken it. It was quite unusual for us to be on the same side of a fence.

Chapter 13

It was well into mid-afternoon before Quintus, Aristo and I headed for the semi public baths near the forum where Quintus assured us that we would find Aronius.   It was one of those club baths favored by the elite who found rubbing elbows with those who actually worked for a living distasteful.   Such establishments, with entrance fees high enough to keep out the riff raff and most of the working classes, had become increasingly popular over the years.

We stripped in the changing room putting our clothing into the care of one of the bathhouse slaves present for that very purpose. Quintus headed directly for the exercise yard while Aristo followed me to the steam room. I wanted a good sweat and scraping down by Aristo's strygil.

The room was rather small but with two tiers of built in benches along walls. It was clouded heavy enough with steam that at first entrance it was difficult to see, and I groped rather blindly up the stepped ledges in order to sit on the upper bench. I was enjoying the heat as my pores began to open. Facing me, two figures broke apart and slid to opposite ends of a bench while in the far corner another couple continued their business. It's funny, the ins and outs of Roman male decorum when it comes to such places. It is perfectly permissible to have a slave doing whatever in the presence of others while the two boys across from me felt obliged to interrupt their pleasure, not, I suspected ,because they were both male but because they were both of a certain social strata.   Had one of them, a particular one indeed, been a slave or even a freedman of the other they could have proceeded without much comment. Finally the one who had first pulled away leaned into the other and whispered something and then he stood and left the steam room. He was followed shortly by the other young man.

"Numerius, is that you?"   The voice of Quintus Aronius came from the far corner where I could see only dimly the figure leaning well back against the wall on the upper tier while another figure, a female who   kneeling on the lower ledge momentarily raised from their manipulations.   Aronius laughed and urged the other figure to continue.

"Are you following me, Numerius?   First dinner and now this?" I could hear the grin in his voice if not see it. He was quite full of himself and puffed up as only ignorance, youth and good looks mixed with equal parts money and entitlement can manage.   Most young men grow out of it. I wondered if Aronius ever would.

"Only to have a word or two, I can assure you of that. Go right ahead. Continue." I could play his game as well. "I just have a few questions for you."

"Only questions?" he asked tapping the head of the slave. "Enough Phoebe, leave us. I'll be safe here with Numerius." Then as the slave girl from the night before removed herself, Aronius placed his hands behind his head and sighed.   "It's rather embarrassing for me Numerius your coming here only in order to ask a few questions.   I had rather supposed that taken with my impressive display of manliness at the dinner last night you'd set out to find me in a swoon of desire. You've hurt my feelings." He moved close enough for us to see each other more clearly and again with that irritating smile that pricked at my memory.

"I am not the type to swoon much, Aronius, as I suspect you're not the type to suffer much from hurt feelings."

"I'm used to having people swoon. It's good for my ego." There was something in the voice that told me he did indeed have people swoon over him, and that he liked it exceedingly well, a young man of conquest, feeling little but keeping score.

"My guess is that your ego is plenty strong enough to withstand my lack of swoon."

He laughed. "Yes, I might be a little big-headed, no pun intended. but I must say that after seeing you fawn all over young Marcus last night at the dinner party, it seems surprising to me that you wouldn't offer me the same attentions. Judging from the slaves you had in attendance I'd be much more your type. I mean Marcus after all ..."

"Are you jealous of Marcus Flavius, Aronius?" I said it trying hard to keep it light and breezy although I found him ever more offensive. Marcus Flavius was supposed to be his friend.

"Don't be absurd, Numerius. Me, jealous of Marcus? Truth is you know, little Marcus would give quite a lot to be where you are right now. He's no match for me. Friends of course but I find it necessary to make sure we're not alone too much, if you know what I mean." He moved closer in an audacious if rather common offering.

"Yes, very, very nice," I said, "but, save it for someone who'll swoon for it. All I have for you are questions."

He looked at me for a moment trying to decide what his reaction should be. He settled on humor. "Oh, all right Numerius, but you had your chance. Now what questions could you possibly have for me?"

"Laelia," I said plainly. Again silence, telling silence. I let the silence sit there.

"Oh, you mean young Marcus's sister don't you?"

"You knew her?"

"Of course. Not well mind you, but Marcus did introduce us."

"Oh come now, my boy. You certainly knew her well enough to give her the bulla, the one I saw you recognize last night on the little slave boy? So don't bother denying it. And a bulla of all things, usually a gift for a baby. I think you knew Laelia quite well indeed."

"I think we've talked enough, Numerius. You offend me with your questions." He stood with what dignity he could muster. He wasn't the actor he supposed.

"I should think it less offensive to answer my questions than those of an overly zealous magistrate. You know how endlessly nosy and tireless they can be, don't you? I don't like going through official channels but I can and will if it becomes necessary." It was totally a bluff on my part but how was he to know?

He thought a moment and then sat back down. "I didn't kill her, Numerius."

"I never said you did." However, at the moment I wasn't convinced. "But you did give her the bulla. Maybe you should tell me about that."

"It was a gift, just a gift."

"A gift to a Vestal? A very pregnant Vestal? Come on man, you'll have to do better than that."

Aronius ran a hand through his wet hair and I suspected that not all the sweat streaming down his body at present was from the effects of the steam. I let him sweat. Sometimes the best way to get a man to talk is silence; all of that void is filled with all kinds of thoughts over which he has no control.

"If, and I say if, Numerius, I participated in such a thing as you seem to imagine, I'd be unwise to admit it, wouldn't I? I mean we all know what happens to Vestals who break their vows and to the men who helped them do so." I have no desire to make my exit from this life in such an unpleasant manner and certainly not at this early date."

"No doubt as Laelia had no desire to be buried alive with only a crust or two of bread and a little water. Not a pretty death, but a long standing tradition for Vestals who stray. Some might argue that in the end it was better for her to go the way she did."

"I didn't do it." He sounded surprisingly convincing.

"Her neck was broken. And, as you've already pointed out to me, you're quite the manly man, quite capable of breaking the fragile neck of such a young lady, especially one who wouldn't be expecting it."

"No, I didn't do it," he insisted. "I swear to the gods."

Maybe he hadn't. My gut suddenly told me probably not. Still a guilty man has been known to lie and I needed to know what I needed to know.

"I'm not big on swearing to the gods, Aronius but I can assure you that as long as you're up front with me your name will not be linked to any of this by me. I'm simply looking for knowledge. Be forthcoming with me and I'll have no reason to go to the authorities. You decide, my way or through the proper channels."

He wiped the sweat from his eyes and head, deciding which way to go. I prayed for him to get on with it before someone else entered the room and broke the spell.

"Tell me all about it, Aronius, from the start," I said in my calmest and most soothing voice. "Tell me the whole story of Aronius and Laelia."

"It's not my fault, at least not in any real way," the young man started. "Marcus set up our meetings, egging me on with hints about how incredibly beautiful how ... untouched she was and ... well, it set up a challenge for me, if you know what I mean." I nodded urging him to go on.

"First it was just harmless flirting, but Marcus kept on telling me that Laelia was pleased and might be open to more, that she deserved more. Those were his actual words, 'she deserved more.' He told me that she was quite unhappy with being a Vestal. At first I just went along with it for the kick of it. How many men have had a chance at bedding a Vestal? And she was quite beautiful as you must know. So, we met once or twice at Marcus' house while his father was out and then at an establishment you know extremely well," he added with a slight smirk of his very attractive mouth. "Somewhere you used to spend a lot of time in, over near the Avertine..."

"I gather you're making reference to the Golden Wing?"

He nodded. "Yes, that's the place. You're a legend there, Numerius or should I say Hylas?"

I let him gloat for a moment before moving on. I now knew what had been bugging Hesperia during our visit that day. As for Aronius, I wanted to hurt him but I wanted the information more. "Ancient history as they say." I grinned back at him. I would be damned if I was going to let this snip of a boy fluster me. "And then..."

"And then she got pregnant. I tried to get her to take care of it, begged her to, but she flatly refused. She said that it was all taken care of. She would have the baby and it would be taken care of. She seemed so sure it would be okay."

"And what about you? Were you so sure?"

"Gods no, I was a nervous wreck, Numerius. Seeing retribution around every corner, but I couldn't sway her. Not her or Marcus. And they're the only other people who knew about it."

"The only ones?" I asked pointedly.

"Except for her slave girl Chloe, but she seemed truly devoted to Laelia. I doubt she would have said anything." I doubted his veracity on the latter but said nothing to that effect.

"And do you know what's become of the faithful Chloe?"

"Haven't seen her since that night."

I sighed, so you were there that night? The night she was killed?"

"But it was early, just to give her the bulla. Marcus thought it would be a touching gesture, just like Marcus coming up with the Romantic notion of giving the baby my bulla."

"But you did it."

"Well, I gave a bulla and I let Marcus and Laelia think it was mine. That's all that mattered to them really. They saw us as some star crossed young lovers."

"And you?"

"Well, I won't lie to you. You wouldn't believe it anyway. I saw myself as a guy who'd gotten lucky with a very attractive Vestal and, having filled the oven, wanted to put the whole thing quietly behind him."

"But not worried enough to kill her?" I asked amazed at this cold recounting of his.

"What would that have accomplished? Like I said, Marcus knew all about it. I would have had to kill them both."

"And the slave." I added.

"And the slave. I may have done a few things some people might find distasteful, Numerius, but murder is not one of them."

"Well, give it time, boy, but for the moment I actually believe you." I did believe it, both contentions, that he hadn't killed Laelia and that he would kill someone along the way eventually. As it happened I was only fifty percent correct. "So, do you have any ideas who might have killed her?"

He shook his head. "No. None. Certainly not Marcus, he hasn't the stuff to do such a thing."

"Her father or yours for that matter? Guarding the family honor or protecting you?"

Aronius snorted. "Maybe hers, if he found out some way, but mine? And certainly not to protect me, Numerius. Anyone who knows my father also knows his opinion of me. Some would have to say he really doesn't like me at all."

I smiled back at him. "Really, I picked you for a spoiled golden haired boy, lavished with every attention."

He grinned back. "And you'd be right, Numerius, but not by my father. My mother, yes, I am without a doubt her fair haired boy. Father's quite a different story. Anything else, Numerius?" He stood once again transformed into the young cock of the walk, the perfect picture of a young Roman nobleman as beautiful and as empty as an old Greek statue.

"Not for now, Aronius. Perhaps some other time. I'll need to talk to you again. But that's all for the time being."

He laughed. "Numerius you continue to disappoint me. I'm beginning to think the stories are all made up and you are not the man once called Hylas." I looked up into his offensive grin. He shook his head and moved slowly toward the door. "I don't think I've ever been turned away twice in the same day. If you should change your mind; let me know and I'll see what I can do if I can still muster any interest."

Obnoxious little bastard I thought giving him enough time to exit and go wherever before leaving myself; besides I could use some quiet time to think about where all this left me.

I sat there longer than I might have. I wanted to be sure I had given Aronius ample time to be involved elsewhere, but finally I stepped out of the heated room and found myself face to face with my faithful Aristo.

"You were in there long enough." Aristo said before I had completely stepped through the door.

"Young Aronius."

"So I saw. He's a vile young man."

"Perhaps but he didn't do it. At least I don't think so."

"That's too bad, I'd rather hoped he was the one and that something dreadful would happen to him."

"Yes, he's a piece of work. I'll give you that, but I don't think he's added murder to his repertoire.   Not yet anyway. He seemed to want to point the finger at old Saddlebags..."

"Uncle," It was Quintus hurrying toward us, his towel loosely wrapped around his waist. He covered the last few feet to us looking like the cat that'd eaten the proverbial canary. "I've found Aronius for you he just jumped in the pool."

'Good job," I grinned and patted his cheek. "But too late. I found him first; by sheer dumb luck, which is how it happens about half the time. Now let's enjoy our bath. Aristo, where is that strigil? Quintus, follow me and I'll fill you in."

After leisurely completing our bath ending with an exquisite massage as only Aristo knew how to give, Quintus and I went home to the house on the Palatine and to check on the slave Apollo. Aristo, on the other hand, insisted on dropping by the new house to see what was being accomplished. I've always been amazed at what that man could get done in a single day. I could use some of that stamina.

Chapter 14

At the door we were met by old Andronicus. "Enter, enter," he whispered excitedly. "It's a miracle. You always bring us good fortune. Go through and see to Apollo. You won't believe it."

I entered the small cubicle where the slave sat on the edge of the bed, bandaged and bruised a bit but not a lot worse for the wear of the previous evening.

"Master," he grinned.

I stopped. The Greek was good. I spoke back in Latin. "So, now you can speak, can you? That is indeed a miracle."

"Yes, a miracle," he answered in quite serviceable Latin.

"I find it hard to believe in miracles, Apollo...or is that your name? Now that you've regained your voice, maybe you have a particular name you'd prefer to be called?"

"No, it is Apollo, Master. It has always been Apollo."

"So tell me more about this so called miracle."

The slave cocked his head to one side whether in a display of hurt or the wish to have me think so. "When I was young I fell from a cart and hit my head against the pavement. When I came to, I could not speak. Then..." He looked up at me through lush eyelashes meant to melt hard hearts. They did indeed have an effect. If my heart was not melted, it was surely softened. "I think the beating I took last night straightened something back out. This morning I could speak. It is the truth, Master."

I would have liked to believe him. He was and is charming, but I have found miracles in my experience to be rather suspect. "Or perhaps you simply thought that being mute was the best way to enter a new household? Perhaps that way you could not talk about things you did not wish to talk about?"

He shook his head. "No, it was the beating. I will swear to it, Master. The Mistress was so pleased. I swear it is..."

"No need to, Apollo. If the household wishes to believe in the miracle...then so be it."

He grinned and as usual the room lightened a little. "The only problem is that she has ordered me to stay here and rest. I am fine and it clears my head to work in the dirt. Talk to her, Master. I could get a lot done before sunset. Just a few of the roselettes perhaps. They should really be gotten in the ground and Andronicus can't manage all alone."

"Andronicus has been managing for years. Don't fret, my friend, he'll collar some poor unfortunate person with not enough to do and then make them miserable helping them out." I smiled. "As for Metella, you obviously haven't been here long if you think any of us stand a chance of changing her orders. No, just stay here and relax. You don't want to fight her, believe me."

The slave sighed and shrugged his shoulders. "As you wish, but at least if you go out again take me with you. After last night, you shouldn't travel alone, Master. I can help there. I have other talents. I wasn't always a gardener. My first owner was into some very shady business on the Avertine. I know how to take care of myself in a brawl. I could be good protection for you. Last night there were eight of them with clubs and weapons. I took out two before that bastard whacked me from the back. If I'd had a caestus or even nice stout stick I could have done a lot better." It was delivered as a matter of fact. He didn't seem to be boasting.

I touched his shoulder and smiled. "You are indeed a multi-talented young man, Apollo. I'll tell you what. You do as Metella says for now and I'll think about it. Fair enough?"

"Fair enough." he replied. "I'll rest. He jumped back to his cot in the corner. "See, I 'm resting already."

We left him to it and went into the garden where Burrus and Metella were enjoying the late afternoon shade of a lovely old plane tree.

"Well, well look who's come home, " Burrus called lifting his wine goblet to us. "Alive and well I see. No broken bones or cracked heads?" He laughed and took a swig of his wine. "Have a seat gents and some of this Pompeii wine you brought me. It's very good by the way, Numerius. Very good indeed." He was in a good mood, probably relieved that Quintus had arrived unassailed and wouldn't have to stand up to Metella's wrath over some bump or bruise. "So Quintus, how's it going my boy? Hard at it?"

"Hard at it, sir," Quintus grinned mischievously. The boy really needed to talk to his father but he seemed to be enjoying the ruse so much I hated to deny him of it.

"Oh, do sit down, you two." Metella spoke unamused by our levity. She looked tired and perhaps a little cross. "We have plenty of time before dinner for a chat and there are a few ground rules we need to go over if Quintus is going to be mucking about in all this." She waited for the two of us to be seated. I knew we were in for it. "Number one is, after the events of last night I find it rather foolish for either of you to go out unaccompanied or unarmed. That won't happen again, until this is over."

There are laws, sister..." I began and was stopped abruptly by a look that could have seared flesh.

" I don't care a fig about the law, Numerius, not when it comes to the safety of my family. Nor would anyone here. Besides we all know there are plenty of ways around it. I'm not fresh in from the country and neither are you. Don't talk to me about laws. You won't be the first to break them. Half the men in Rome carry some sort of weapon. Don't be a dolt. So, unless you are giving up on this business completely you will abide by that rule. Agreed?"

Quintus looked at me. I looked at Burrus who shrugged and turned back to Metella. "Agreed."

"And now as for going out alone," Metella began as if checking off a market list...

"Ah, on that point I have something I've been meaning to talk to you about." I launched into Apollo's offer and we continued down Metella's check list until, mercifully, dinner was announced.

At dinner Lucia was wearing the coral pendant and earrings I had brought for her. Very pretty indeed and for the first time I envisioned her as more than a young girl. Soon they would be talking about her marriage no doubt. Time moves too quickly as you reach your middle years. It seemed only yesterday that she and Quintus were grubby, leaky nosed marble crawlers. Now suddenly here was Quintus beginning to work with me and Lucia turning into some lucky young man's potential wife. I myself would soon be turning forty. It seemed impossible, but there it was. We spend all our youth rushing into adulthood, careers, pleasure of all kinds and accomplishments of rather lackluster merit and then finally wake up to the fact that we've gone through the half of it without really paying attention. For a while I was quiet and let the others chatter, taking in for myself what I had of family. Even Burrus held a place in my heart that night. After the ladies left us Burrus, Quintus and I sat long over more of the gifted wine pleasantly talking into the night. It has become one of my favorite memories.

Toward dawn the house was awakened. I sat upright groggy and slow to respond. I never woke early. I heard shouting and bare feet slapping across marble floors, Burrus cursing, Quintus's voice.

"I'll kill the sons of bitches, " came the boom of Burrus enraged voice over that of the others.

I threw on a tunic and headed for the hubbub. Lamps were being lit and half dressed slaves were running back and forth with bowls of water, bindings and wine. By the time I reached the atrium it was already full with Burrus, Quintus and Apollo seated on chairs or benches while Metella ,grim faced bathed a wound above the eye of Quintus and Aristo, calm as always, bathed a similar bruise on Burrus, half the slaves running and fetching and the other half rooted in place, watching.

"You'll kill no one this morning Quintus Lucius," Metella said sternly to her husband. "What on earth were you doing out at this hour anyway?"

"If they want to play hard ball we can too. By the gods the three of us made a proper showing. They'll think twice before trying us again. I swear I heard the arm of one of the bastards crack like a nut when Apollo there got hold of em. He came bounding out the door at the first scuffle. Nice work, very nice work," he called toward the slave whose knuckles were being bathed by another slave. "Wasting his time as a gardener, that boy. Jupiter, it was great."

Metella finishing with Quintus pushed Aristo aside and applied a vinegar soaked cloth to a particularly nasty cut over her husband's eye and none too gently. "Great you say. The three of you banged up, marked up and bleeding . How exactly do you call that great, Quintus Lucius?"

Burrus grinned up at her, ex soldier and old war horse that he was and took her hand gently in his big bear of a paw. "You should see them, my dear. Their ladies and flunkies will be doing a lot more bandaging and tending than this, by a hell of a lot. Threaten me, in front of my own house? Let them try."

"Shh now, Burrus. " I noticed she had slipped back to his cognomen a good sign for us all. "Enough, settle down.   The whole house is in an uproar. I'll talk to you later about breaking the rules within hours of our agreement. We need to get people seen to and back to bed now.

"I couldn't sleep if I had to," Burrus said smiling broadly and testing a variety of bruises with his finger tips. "Damn, I haven't had so much fun since I left the army."

"Yes dear, but enough now." Metella patted the top of her husband's head as one would a small boy's and then moved on to her son who was now being attended to by Aristo. "Here, now let me see," she said pushing the slave deftly aside. "Take a look at Apollo. I'll finish this."

It took a while to finish the job to her satisfaction; longer to put the house back to bed and closing in to dawn when the three of us sat alone in the beginning hour of day's light in the atrium..

"Someone wants you out of this, Numerius," Burrus said biting into a slab of cheese and ripping off the end of a fresh loaf of bread. "You've certainly ruffled someone's feathers, my boy."

"The question is whose? What exactly did they say?"

"Well, exactly. This big hot shot of a would be bully got right up in my face and said 'Tell that...'" he looked cautiously at Metella, "...blank blanking aging whore to give it up before someone really gets hurt."

I swallowed not needing him to fill in the blanks for me.

"Oh yeah, and something else. He called you Hylas. That was it exactly...Hylas, that aging whore."

"Well the aging part was certainly unkind..." I said trying for humor.

"Hylas? Who still calls you that, Numerius? Shouldn't that help?"

I shrugged. "Not many, not to my face anyway. On the other hand people have long memories when it comes to scandal. There are plenty about who might know of my past."

Burrus snorted. "Hell, man, half of Rome's heard about your past," Burrus looked as pleased as a slave boy with a plate of honey cakes. "And half of that half probably knows from first hand experience." Thank you Burrus, I thought. At least he was enjoying himself. "The point is, woman, that old Hy... I mean Numerius has stepped on some toes here. Pretty big toes I should say and when that happens...well when they start squawking this loudly at you you're pretty close to home. So tell us, Numerius, whose toes are you stepping on? Let's plant a foot a little higher up and see what they think."

"The problem is I don't know who it is."

"Who might it be?" Metella asked, not happy to accept the whole scenario.

"Well, someone connected to this of course by involvement or for hire. As Burrus has so graciously pointed out for us there are plenty of people who know about my past." I didn't mention Marcus's father, Old Saddlebags. Specifics are never comfortable when it comes to talking of my past and I didn't see where either of the two needed to know about that.

"Just the truth, brother." Burrus grinned and tore off another piece of bread. The events certainly hadn't affected his appetite. "Just stating the facts." The fact that he called me brother was a sign of approval from him that I had heard exactly once before in the 18 years since the birth of their first child. The old bugger was really enjoying this.

"What about Pausina?" Metella asked thoughtfully.

"She's chief Vestal for the gods sake Metella," brayed Burrus, "and a woman to boot."

"And I would ask myself what kind of chief Vestal gets herself mixed up in some secret investigation anyway. I'd put her high upon the list, Numerius. Mark my words. She should have gone straight to the authorities, but she chose to contact you and set you snooping about in secret. Don't trust women who do things secretly, Numerius. I wouldn't."

She was right. I didn't want to admit it but Pausina had to go on the list, along with Saddlebags and maybe even Hesperia, definitely Aronius's father. Yes, Pausina would have to go up high on that list. The thought came as an unpleasant surprise to me, but the lady knew something. I needed to find out what exactly and how far, if any, she was involved in it. Hesperia also needed to be on the high part of that list. As I have known from experience when you share a bed with the powerful of Rome you have more access to secrets than can be healthy for you; and when you manage those who do, the secrets multiply exponentially. I needed to talk to Aristo and come up with a plan. It would be a busy day. I would have several calls to make.

"Well, enough for now, but I'll trust you to work it out, Numerius. Now, if you'll pardon us I've got to drag our illustrious warrior here off to bed for a little sleep. You might do the same as it's still too early for anything else. And wherever you go, you take Apollo with you. Understand?" I nodded. "Come it's bed time for you." she said standing and offering her hand to her husband.

He rose with an alacrity I hadn't seen him display in years. "Ah yes, but I warn you I'm not sleepy in the least, Lady, not in the least."

"Oh don't be a fool, Burrus. But come and we shall see."

It did me good to watch the two of them like that, still in love. There were few times I could be fond of Burrus, but this morning was one of them.

Chapter 15

In the end I decided the first visit should be to Hesperia. We set off early, far before the hour Hesperia would normally have risen. It is often good to talk to a person at a time when they are not functioning at their best. For some that may be late at night, for many while they're drinking and for others, like Hesperia, it's first thing in the morning. I was accompanied this morning by Aristo and Apollo and, per Metella's orders, we weren't exactly unarmed as to the letter of the law. Aristo carries and uses the curved thin double-edged Syrian dagger well and Apollo carried a hefty set of street caestus unlike any found in a legitimate boxing match but quite useful when quickly slipped onto the hands of a man wanting to inflict serious damage. These had been provided for Apollo from the old gear of Burrus and were easily concealed on his person. Quintus we had left home as his bruises from the night before were a bit obvious and would certainly have raised comments of a sort I wanted to avoid today.

Few customers arrive at the Golden Wing so early in the day. And Apollo's knock on the barred door took longer than usual to be answered. I stated my name and business and the slave who had not recognized me but certainly knew me by name slid the bolt open and let us through. We waited in a pleasant side room while a message was sent to Hesperia. If my guess was right and they had to wake her we might be waiting a while. Hesperia had never been too friendly in the early morning hours. There was very little action going on around us except for slaves who did the cleaning and polishing up. One of them, a not so young girl from the far reaches of Gaul judging by her flaxen hair, with an ample bosom which threatened to spill over the cut of her tunic was finding herself hard pressed to keep her eyes on her work and off Apollo. As for Apollo, he bloomed under the scrutiny.

After a reasonable period of time a young Greek slave whose innocent beauty belied his surroundings approached us and ferried the message that Hesperia couldn't come down so early but I could come up to her rooms if it were important. I said that would be fine, and left Apollo and Aristo to their own devices while I followed the boy up to my old apartments. She had redone them of course. Hesperia was always fond of flash with too many colors for my taste and too many statues of various styles, sizes and quality. It looked like a brothel which of course it was. Still, I liked to think that in my day it had had more style.

"There aren't many men I'd drag myself from bed for, not at this hour anyway. What's so important, Hylas?" Though this greeting was not exactly in the manner expected by the patron-client relationship we shared, it was not at all bad for Hesperia. We had been friends and competitors long before I had been given my freedom and eventually bought the place lock stock and barrel.

"We need another chat. And no leaving out the bits and pieces this time, Hesperia." I sat down in a chair and motioned to another. "Time for the truth."

She pulled her heavy hair from where it fell over her shoulders trying to decide just how much to tell me. I felt rather confident she already knew what it was about.

"All right. Have at it and let me get back to bed. You know I love you, but business is business, Hylas. At least that's what you always told me."

I nodded. "And so it is, but this is the business that you have because of me, but enough of all that. I simply want to know about Marcus Flavius and Quintus Aronius, especially the latter. And this time, Hesperia, do try to tell me everything."

She bit her lip and looked at her nails, then sighed. "Oh, okay. Marcus I hardly know. I suspect he is a bit light in the purse to come here often. From time to time he comes with older, shall we say more established men. Young Aronius on the other hand is quite the regular, well thought of by the staff, both the girls and the boys, generous, quite the philanderer but nevertheless he is quite the darling young man, charming everyone." She stopped for a moment to look at me and judge my reaction. "But that's not what you really want to know, is it?"

I shook my head and stifled the desire to question Aronius' being charming in anyone's eyes ... but the matter was not to the point. So, I went on. "No, I want to know what you didn't want to tell me the other day." I suppose it was only to be expected of her to wonder if I had softened up enough to let the matter slide at some generalities. I hadn't and she saw it.

"For nigh on to a year now he's been meeting someone here. And no, I don't know who the lady is, Hylas. So don't ask. It's all very secretive. She arrives very covered up and no one but his personal slave is allowed near their room until the lady is gone. The slave girl of the woman in quesiton however is called ..."

"Chloe" I provided for her.

"Yes, that is it. So, there you have it, Hylas. You obviously know who the lady is. Now I don't suppose you'd like to tell me?"

"Some things are better not to know Hesperia," I said, my voice heavy with impression. I saw her take it in. She checked her nails again. Thinking.

"In that case... Maybe there's one more bit you should know, Hylas. About once a month someone comes with money to deposit on Aronius's account. Again, no, I don't know who. It's delivered by a slave, obviously well placed, with simple instructions to post the funds to the boy's account. The funds are, shall we say, very liberal. Young Aronius can afford to be generous here. The boy seemed quite surprised the first time or two when he was informed of this substantial credit, but that soon ended and now he takes it for granted.'"

"And no idea at all who sends the cash?" I asked even though she'd previously denied it.

"No." There came the nails again. "None."

I suspected she didn't know but I also suspected she had an idea or two about who it might be. I gave her a moment to see if she'd go down that road. She didn't.

'Well then, Hesperia," I stood and opened my arms in an offer of embrace. "I'll let you get back to bed now. And thank you for being straight with me this time."

She rose and gave me a hug. "Anytime, Hylas. I know I owe you a lot. I hope I've been helpful." She did her best to sound sincere, and I've been around too long to hope for better.

Once out of the Golden Wing we headed toward the forum. "And what did the two of you learn?" I asked Aristo and Apollo. The younger slave blushed and grinned. Aristo grimaced.

"He learned nothing except for how to carry on with a washer woman. A waste of time and energy," spat Aristo.

"Never a waste," said Apollo defensely. "You're the one who told me to ask questions."

"I can just imagine the questions you were asking. I could hear the two of you going at it in the next room, I don't know why you bothered to leave the room." Aristo was in his prim mode. I've never been successful at breaking him away from it.

"She was noisy I'll admit, but I did learn that young Quintus Aronius comes often, seems to have unlimited credit, plays and flirts with everyone but sleeps mostly with the girls and lady friends who arrive wrapped up in pallas concealing their faces. All fine figured. And that once old Quintus Aronius, his father, showed up and had quite a shouting match with the boy. Probably over all the money he spends."

"Scratch that last bit, Old Aronius doesn't pay. Seems young Aronius has a secret financier for his excursions here. Still an interesting point, and not a bad hour's work, Apollo. "

Aristo set his lips in a tight line while Apollo beamed. "Ah, let the boy have some fun, Aristo. We all have our ways of getting at what we want to know."

We left the center and headed out across the forum to the Quirinal and the house of Marcus Flavius. I hoped to speak to both father and son this time.

We were left waiting at the door for some time. The door slave returned with two muscle boys in tow. "The master will see you in his study." the old guy said. "The others must remain here." I nodded in agreement and one of the bully –boys stayed with Aristo and Apollo while the other followed me and the door slave back into the house.

He did not ask me to be seated. "I did not wish to see you, Meridius. I had hoped to avoid ever laying eyes on you again."

"So why did you?" I asked the old bugger. He sat looking at me from across his writing table for all the world looking like a statue of some dried up ancient senator of the Republic.

"You will not see my son again for any reason. I don't approve of his 'hob-nobbing' with the likes of you."

I felt my ears burning but bit my tongue trying to keep my goal in mind. My facial expressions alas were less governable.

"Whatever foolishness and stupidity I did as a young man is not the question here. I have renounced my youthful indiscretions and luckily recovered from them." The old man spitted his angry words at me. "My son, as I am sure you are well aware, already leans toward indulgence and as his father it is my job to see that he slips no further into this mire of filth. You will not see him again. You will not correspond with him in any manner, or I shall bring you up on charges of corruption. Oh yes. I know about your disgusting little dinner episode. If Marcus couldn't be counted on to be entirely forthcoming you can be assured that his slave's tongue was adequately loosened. My son and I have come to an understanding, on my terms. He, like everyone, will pay a price for his faults. I can assure you of that. I have forbidden him further contact with you, your nephew, that Aronius and the rest of that crowd attending your debauch of a dinner. I will drag you all through the mud, including my son if need be. Do you understand me on these points?"

I wanted to lash out at the pompous hypocritical old bastard. "Yes. I think I do." I meant to stop there but couldn't help myself. "You don't love me anymore. I'm broken hearted, Saddlebags." It did my heart good to see the old bugger turn purple with apoplexy rage. So I'd blown my chance for any follow up questions. It had been worth it. Nothing angers me more than old clients who suddenly find themselves too respectable to acknowledge even the possibility, even in private, that at one point in their lives they had enjoyed themselves in my company . I hoped that the old pompous clod would choke on his rage and for a moment it looked as if I might get my wish, but he recovered.

"I have one question and one only, Hylas. Do you or do you not know who murdered my daughter?"

I wondered if he were aware of the fact that he had used my old name. I smiled. "I do not, but I will; and when I do, you can be sure that you will be the last to know."

"Get out." he shouted, again standing and leaning across the table, turning once again that lovely shade of purple. "Vorax, get in here and take this, this thing back to the streets where he came from."

The bully boy, Vorax, must have been waiting right outside the door because he was heading me out of the room before old Saddlebags had finished and surprisingly gently given the attitude he was striking. Once the door was close behind us, he eased up even more and slowed our pace considerably.

"I don't know what stick you jabbed up the ass of the old man back there, but I'm certainly not too goody-two-shoes to be seen with you. If you know what I mean." He grinned, not unattractively. "I don't have the money of course.. but if you ever needed..."

"Information?" I asked with my warmest smile. "We might come to an agreement of some sort?"

He grinned.

"Then, on account, is the boy here? Could I see him?"

"Not a chance.   The young one took off this morning just before dawn. In quite the hurry, I might add. Unusual for him to be up before noonday."

"I would like to know where he went and when he returns. I will get in touch."

The bully-boy nodded and grinned. "Just send the word and we'll work something out."   I nodded and then we were at the outside door and his manner reverted to what would be expected and perhaps reported by the other bruiser. Having received the information I wanted to know about the boy, I trusted I would not have to see either of the bully boys again, but Vorax was lined up if for some reason I needed him. Had I been a coarser person I would have spit on the house of the Flavii as we departed. I did not, but I was not happy.

Our trip back to the Palatine would be quicker than our previous sojourn as I was stirred on by anger. I said little except for a most cursory report on the proceedings. Old Saddlebags had definitely screwed with my mood. "Pompous old crab," I muttered under my breath. "The boy is evidently not there, having shot out of the house before dawn this morning," I said to no one in particular. "Now where has he gotten to so bright and early? That's what I would like to know; not the time for a young Roman about town to be going out, although getting home would be different." That might well be normal for the likes of the Aronius crowd; many a young Roman reached home as his parents were rising.

Flavius, anxious to be in that particular crowd would be no different. His going out though, was quite a different story. Something at the pit of my gut told me it had something directly or indirectly connected to what I wanted to know. The question was where had he gone? Certainly not off to see young Aronius...that would have been futile at such an early hour. Pausina's? I doubted it, she herself had said he really couldn't afford the place and even if it were for other reasons, why so early? A more reasonable departure time would have suited just as well. Somewhere out of Rome was the only thing that made sense. but where and why?

Chapter 16

I needed to make a trip out to the Janiculum and the Aronius place but after our rounds this morning I wasn't about to do it on foot. I'd had enough walking for one day and places on that particular hill could be quite a distance. We'd have to swing by the house on the Palatine and haul out the litter. No more hired litter bearers for the time being. Hired bearers have nothing to lose but their fare if their passengers are attacked as long as they don't interfere nor was there much to gain if they decided to get involved.

By the time we reached the house I had worked off much of my anger. While the litter was readied, we had time for a cool drink in the garden with Metella. She was fully engaged now. Be careful before threatening a she-wolf's cub. Metella was out for blood.

"So where was the boy?" she asked point blank. "I don't trust that entire family. Where could he have been at those hours if what the body guard said was true? And why do they need those louts of body guards suddenly? That old man is up to something, Numerius. You can count on it. From what you've told me those were hired thugs or ex-gladiators not slaves of the household. He has brought in special forces and that bodes ill."

"We too have taken our precautions," I reminded her gently.

"Nonsense. It's not at all the same. We were threatened. We prepared to protect ourselves. Are you telling me Flavius with his household and estates couldn't find ample 'protection'? No, it smacks of something more. You hire thugs to get things done. Things you don't want to sully your own hands with.

"Mark my words that old geezer has a plan and it's not to sit idly by up in his house on the Quirinal and wait for it all to happen around him. He's in play now. He has a plan, a plan of action."

She had a point. There had been no body guards on my first trip up the hill and things had certainly heated up around our investigation, perhaps heat was being applied to old Flavius as well.

"Do you honestly believe he didn't know she was pregnant? How could that be? How could a mother and father not know? This may be Rome but the Quirinal is not that far from the house of the Vestals. You can't tell me that any mother would not have taken the time to see her daughter and having seen her, to notice she was with child; the father I suppose, it's possible. Men can be such blind idiots, but not a mother."

"I haven't talked to the mother."

Metella arched an eyebrow. "Well, perhaps you should, Numerius. The woman of the household is the only person who knows more about what is going on under her roof than the slaves. You want knowledge? Ask the slaves or the Domina. Any fool knows that."

I chuckled. "Of course you're right, dear sister, and the slaves we can often get to. The mistress of the house, well, that's a different story."

"Don't placate me, Numerius. Find a way to get to the mother and you'll find she has a wealth of information. She probably knows twice the amount of what her husband and son are up to than they do themselves. Get to her."

I smiled and nodded. "I've no doubt you're right, but the question is how to get to her, a woman of her standing. You don't just walk up, bang on the door and demand to see the Mistress of a house."

"Oh come now, Numerius," she snorted. "You're supposed to be the investigator here. Are you so overwhelmed by the idea of respectable women that you can't see reality? They come and go like anyone else. They shop, they see people, they go places. Use your head! There are ways to get to them."

Luckily for me Apollo stuck his head through the pillars to motion to us that Aristo had returned with the large litter and all was ready to head up to the Janiculum. I nodded in agreement with Metella, thanked her and beat a hasty retreat before she pinned my ears back any further. Aristo and I climbed into the litter. Apollo, the bulky, armed and at our side along with my own well-muscled and well trained litter bearers, and we began the uphill journey to see Aronius.

it was not easy going. The house of Aronii was situated on the Janiculum among the newly built private homes which seemed more like country villas than the houses of Rome proper. It was quite a work-out for our guys. I would have to remember to reward them with a special treat of some kind. It kept them happy and ready to go that extra mile for me when asked. Fairness goes a long way with slaves.

The gates of the villa stood open. We started up the crushed stone drive past the carefully tended grounds alive with workers who paid scant attention to us. We were met at a small but lovely little building, obviously placed there for the purpose, by a guard of sorts who sent a slave boy scurrying to the house proper with our request for a visit. In the meantime, we were invited to sit in the comforting shade of an old and gracious plane tree while our litter bearers were offered cool water to soothe parched throats by another little slave. I was impressed with Aronius's thoughtfulness for uninvited and unexpected guests. I looked around with pleasure at the set-up. Perhaps I had been wrong about the new house; perhaps I should have built a place up here further from the hustle and bustle of the center with more room to spread out and breathe fresh air. It was lovely and the sentiment sweet, but not for me. Too far from the center for me. I'd have been pacing like a caged lion in the arena in a matter of days. I knew that and accepted it as so, however lovely the pictured bliss might be. It was exactly the type of thing Aristo might envision for us, but it would never work for me.

"What are you smiling at?" Aristo interrupted my thoughts.

"Just thinking what a lovely place."

"In two days you'd be bored stiff up here," Aristo said flatly. "But yes, it's lovely."

I laughed. He knew me too well. We'd never live in a place like this; but I could guarantee him the wherewithal to do so when I slipped over the river Styx, and that made me happy. Money goes a long way toward happiness despite what the cynics say.

I caught sight of the little slave heading toward us from the house as fast as his tanned little legs could carry him. Time to turn back to the business at hand.

"Come, Aristo," I said rising from my seat. "We're about to move."

The little slave boy arrived grinning and barely breathing hard. "The master says bring them up. Bring them up," he repeated to the guard slash gate keeper.

"So do it, boy," he grinned back at the boy. "Slowly though, not everyone enjoys running the way you do." He patted the boy's head fondly and turned to us. The boy will lead you the way, Sirs. He's a good boy."

"Any fool could see that," I said smiling at the boy.

"The boys are both high spirited like their mother," the guard smiled and patted the boy on his head. I looked once more at the boys. I knew those shiny faces, those dancing eyes.

"Their mother? I asked. "Head on, young man," I said while Aristo tipped the man and slid me another coin to give the boy. "Lead on." I held the coin out to him and enjoyed watching his dark eyes widen. He looked toward the man in question for permission.

"It's all right.   You may take it, Ajax." The man laughed and winked at the happy boy.

Then he nodded toward me. "Her name is Phillipia, Sir." He smiled softly and waited just a moment for me to put it together. She used to work for you, Sir and I used to sneak in to see her when my master visited the" ....he stopped and casting his eyes on the boys, continued with a wink "your place of business."

"Phillipia is here?"

"Yes, sir, she is here. My master bought her just after you left for Pompeii. He knew we had feelings for each other and he is kind."

"He is indeed," I said thinking the price he would have paid for one of the girls from the Golden Wing. "And very generous. Your name?"

"Calyx," he smiled. "Phillipia still talks about you. She says you too were kind. She will be excited to know of your visit."

"She is happy?" I asked placing a hand on the slave's shoulder. He grinned back at me. "I certainly like to think so, Sir. Perhaps she will be able to tell you herself. Agamemnon, run find

Mamma and tell her old master is here and Ajax take these gentlemen to the house."

"Now, go, boys." We headed up the crushed stone pathway toward the big house where we were handed over to another slave who led us through a beautiful atrium and into the study of Aronius the elder. He was nothing at all like the man I had expected from having met his son.

Aronius, well fed and just this side of plump, jumped up from his chair as we entered. "Gentlemen, gentlemen, what can I do for you this fine day?" he cried all smiles and flowing warmth. "They tell me you have some questions for me. Not that I'm one people often come to for answers, but come, sit and ask away. I'll gladly be of what help I can."

He was older to be sure, but I did seem to remember him. His smile reminded me...a regular customer of two years or more just before I retired. He had always kept a low profile staying away from our flashier wares, interested more in the pretty slave girl next door. He had been well liked by the staff.

"Is it about the boy? Has he got himself in over his head again? He is too excessive although I've tried everything I know to counteract....Well....His mother... well,she dotes on him you know. Her only son." His face hardened in anticipation. "So tell me, what is it this time?" He finished and indicated again that we should sit. We did, and he himself sat across from us looking somewhat like a nervous school boy now that he had stopped talking. He wrung his hands. "What's the brat done now?" The change of tone surprised me.

"I don't know that he's done anything amiss..." I began but was stopped by a wave of his hand.

"No need to take it easy on me, Hylas. I know you. I know the Golden Wing, used to be one of your regular customers, now not so much. Quintus on the other hand would live at the place if he could afford it. He can't. We've rowed about it before, but nothing stops him. Where he gets the means I'm afraid to ask. The boy is trouble, I know that. So tell me what kind it is this time and I will do what I can."

I suddenly felt sorry for the man. By all judgment he appeared decent and good, kindly disposed to all and to have a son like young Aronius must have been a galling blow to him.

"Your son might not even be..." I began trying to soften the way.

"My son," he interrupted bitterly, "is most likely to be involved in whatever shenanigans are happening around him. Unfortunately he is most often the leader in them. No, I have no illusions about that young man and I shudder to think what sort of man he will turn out to be if he lives long enough. So tell me, my friends, what is it this time? What has Quintus got himself mixed up in?"

He looked at us blankly. No doubt he had had several of these visits before. I could forgive him the bitterness that crept through his voice and eyes for it is indeed a bitter thing when one you have cared for and encouraged, lavished attention on day after day turns away from all you have tried to instill and takes the opposite path. I have seen it with the people I've worked with over the years. I still remember the betrayal and hurt. How much more must this man feel when the person in question is a son?

"Do you happen to know where your son was ..." I began gently.

"Ah, Sir, I wont be able to help you there." He interrupted me again with a wave of his hand. "I rarely know where my son is unless I have him followed and I used to do that occasionally until it proved disappointing beyond words. I would imagine he was out whoring or getting drunk with his friends. Just what is all this about? Something about your approach tells me this is not just another brawl, another foolish prank. It does not surprise me. You may speak freely. This is serious, isn't it?"

I shifted on my chair and decided to tell him. "It's about a murder." He bit his lip. Deep in his eyes there was a flash of some feeling I could not decipher but he said nothing. We let the words hang there for a moment. "A young woman, high born, and a missing child. I'm afraid I'm not at liberty to supply you with her name..."

Aronius sighed as he dropped his shoulders. His eyes filled with tears and placing both hands on his knees he stared momentarily at the painted ceiling. He took a breath. "Would it be the Vestal Laelia?"

I said nothing but nodded slightly.

"We of course heard of her death, but nothing of a child."

"As you no doubt are aware, no one would want that information out Quintus Aronius. I should warn you of that."

He straightened a little. "What Rome has become these days. It frightens me for the future, Numerius, isn't it now? Numerius something Pulcher, isn't that right?" He halted questioningly.

"Meridius," I supplied.

He nodded, "That's it. Meridius. Numerius Meridius Pulcher. It use to be plain Hylas. Those were simpler days, Numerius. At least for me they were. It didn't seem all that complicated when I was a boy. We caroused, drank and whored like all privileged young men of those times, but there was no real harm done. Now its ladies of good family and Vestal virgins. Where will it end, my friend? We are Rome and look at what we're becoming. This emperor has raised Tigellinus to the highest levels. That kind of man is who has the care of Rome in his hands. It doesn't bode well for us."

" I sat stock still, afraid to interrupt his monologue, afraid for him if he talked like this where he might be heard by others.

He sighed again and seemed to come back to the present. "My son knew the Vestal. Her slave girl Chloe has on several occasions over the last year or so delivered messages to him here. I suspected the affair but had heard nothing of a child. You say the child is missing?"

"It would be your grandchild..." I started but was stopped.

"No, not mine. Not mine at all, Numerius. I know that may sound harsh but...well things are not what they always appear as you well know. No, not my grandchild." he stopped again blinking for a moment before continuing in a softer vein. My wife..we were not making the family we had hoped for. The gods did not favor us. Her first three pregnancies ended in miscarriage. Then finally a little boy, the sweetest little thing you could have imagined was born to us. He died less than two years later. It broke Helena's heart. She was never the same. To me or to anyone. She refused to try again and I could not blame her. I knew what those dead children had cost her. I could not ask her to suffer it again. She had suffered enough.

"But Quintus?"

"Quintus is not mine, nor hers, not naturally. He was brought to us almost a year to the day after our son had died. You should have seen her. There was no way I could have refused her that child. Even had I known how he would turn out I doubt I would have refused her. He was the first speck of life in her eyes since the day we lost our own son. I couldn't have said no. So here we are. I can't tell you where the child came from exactly. Only that he was high born. I have taken an oath and I will not break it now, but as I will point out, you are running in high circles, Numerius. Dangerous circles. So, my friend," he said as he stood. "What I can tell you is... my so-called son was indeed with the lady in question. As for the child, well, I would not be surprised if it were his, but if you're thinking he's whisked it away somewhere for himself...Well, he's far too selfish for that. Finally, whether he committed the murder, I simply have no idea. I would hope that he would at least be incapable of that, but presently I would not like to swear to it. And now, if you will excuse me. I really need some time to ... to think and decide where we go from here. I wish I had more facts to give you. I don't, but should I find out more about what actually happened surrounding this mess , I'll get word to you."

I stood to meet him. "You know, he may be completely innocent of this." I said trying to offer a little hope.

"You are kind to offer hope, Numerius. But it is too late...far too late. He may be innocent of it, as you say, but there is no way he is innocent in it, is there? Far from it I fear. I've known for some time where the boy is headed...the question is how quickly he will arrive there."

It was not the interview I had expected. There was no need to offer false platitudes. The man knew the boy and where he was headed in life. It was Helena, the wife the old man hurt for. He was dreading the day he would not be able to keep what the lad was from his mother. I thanked him again and we were let out by Aronius himself. The slave boy, Ajax, met us and escorted us back to the litter.

"Master.." the soft mellifluous voice came from under the shade tree and I turned to see Phillipia. She had matured, most certainly, but I easily recognized the lovely young gamine of years past.

"Phillipia," I said smiling. I stepped into the shade to greet her. You look lovely. Life here agrees with you?"

"I am very happy master what with Calyx and the boys." Her eyes shone with obvious pride. "The master here has been very good to us."

"You remember Aristo, no doubt." I asked aware that he'd come up behind me.

Her smile broadened. "How could I forget? I had quite a crush on him when I first came to the Golden Wing, but even then I think he had his heart set on someone else?" She smiled at me again. "Then, I found Calyx and I have never really looked back. Although I have wondered from time to time," she said with a grin directed not at me."

"You are still lovely, my girl and had I not already given my heart, you'd have found me more than willing." Aristo grinned back and ducked his head shyly. I made a mental note to ask him more about this at a future time. There was obviously a story to be heard here.

"And the master's son, young Quintus, How is he?" I watched the shadow come over her face, more telling than the words that followed. "Young Quintus is not his father."

She said no more but I got the message and I knew from the past what it felt like to watch a future master, one dreaded, draw nearer and nearer his ownership of you. There would be much lamenting in this household when the old man came to his end. "Quintus Aronius seems a hearty man. May he live a long life!"

"As the gods will it, my Lord." Phillipia smiled again. It was good to see you again sir. May the fates be kind to you."

"And to you," I said motioning to Aristo to hand over the money bag he carried. "Here take this and apply it to your pecunium. Perhaps you need never worry about that future day."

"Sir," she said holding the bag to her chest. We are in your debt. We have been saving; for the boys when they become of age. We should like to see them free. We are grateful to you and shall include you in our prayers." She dropped to her knees and bowed her head.

"May the Fates be kind," I repeated and touched the top of her lovely hair. "It has been good to see you again."

We turned and got into the litter and headed back down the drive. The boys, Ajax and Agamemnon ran with us, laughing all the way to the gate. Inside the litter we were silent for some time. Then Aristo spoke. "We could perhaps do something for Phillipia and her brood," he said in a carefully controlled voice. "She should not have to worry about the day when Young Aronius takes over.

It was rare that Aristo spoke to me thus and it was obvious that he had strong feelings about the matter. "Perhaps you can look into it," I said laying my hand on his. "Let's see what we can do." We continued back down the Janiculam in silence, Aristo thinking his thoughts and I contemplating just who might be the natural father of young Quintus. There was a story there that needed to be unearthed.

We'd made the long languid journey home in the heat of the Roman day, or nearly so, when we were stopped. The litter came to an abrupt halt and we were set down on the pavement. I parted the curtains which we had closed against the hot sun. Blocking our path were several officious looking guards, not your common group, but well polished and armed.

"Numerius Meridius Pulcher," Called out the obvious leader of the group, a severe but good looking man with riveting eyes that took me in at a glance; "You are to come with us," he said as I stepped out and stood up on the pavement.

"And may I ask by whose authority?" I said pulling myself up to face him squarely. Bravado is often worth a try, but my gut didn't really buy into it this time. This felt bad.

"Do not make us drag you there, Meridius. Come easily and your attendants may go on their way unharmed. It is your choice." He looked coolly into my face and I knew we didn't want to mess with the alternatives.

"I will go with you," said Aristo coming from the litter behind me.

"No," the guard and I said at the same time. "You go home and tell them what has happened," I continued alone. "Let Metella know I may be a bit late for dinner." I tried to sound unconcerned but doubted I carried it off very well.

"But..." Aristo began.

"Do as I say, Aristo."

The guard motioned and a closed litter came from around the corner. "We have arranged for your transport. Please get in."

I nodded in agreement and turned to look at Aristo and my litter bearers for what I sincerely hoped would not be the last time. Aristo stood stoutly biting his lip trying and failing to look reassuring. I tried the same then climbed into the closed litter, a nasty wooden and leather thing which provided not the merest crack from which to see the outside.

Chapter 17

We didn't go far. Even in the closed litter I could mentally trace our path and be reasonably sure of where we were. My escort was not making any pretense of trying to confuse me. We headed straight down the street and turned right, then left and started up the incline that lead to the old palace and its surrounding palaces now used for official business. Not a place one liked to be taken under armed escort. I had definitely stepped on some toes, maybe some I would regret. I was relieved that they had not allowed Aristo to come. At least he would be safe if I had indeed gone too far. As a rule, I rarely sweat, but I could feel it now, gathering beneath my arms and over my lip. Nothing raises fear in one as present danger which while recognized as imminent is currently unknown. I like to be prepared beforehand. You can keep your surprises.

We were let in a gate and the litter was set down. My guard, the one with the eyes, pulled back the leather curtain, kind enough to offer me a hand out of the litter and onto the pavement. Fear is better met on your feet than reclining in a litter and I was grateful to be on mine. "Thank you," I said looking squarely into the man's face. He said nothing but I thought I detected the slightest upturn of the corner of his mouth, not a smile exactly, but not entirely unfriendly. If I were to be summarily clamped into prison or done away with, this guy didn't know about it. It gave me hope.

My guard led me to another door, past the posted guards and into a cool marble hallway dominated by a beautiful pool complete with fountain. It certainly didn't look like a prison. We turned a corner and arrived at a door flanked by more guards. My guard saluted them. "By his order."

One of the guards looked me over carefully as my guard turned and retreated down the hallway from which we had come. "Tigellinus never ceases to surprise us, eh Macro?" the guard said to his cohort. "Go ahead take him in."

My distaste of the way he stressed the pronoun was balanced by the name he had used. Tigellinus and I had a past history that suddenly promised some hope that this was not what I had imagined. I was led through the doors and down another long hallway, this one bright with sunlight. The guard led me silently to a single door at the end of the hallway, knocked twice, opened the door and gently directed me through it. It was dark.

Tigellinus, or at least who I supposed was Tigellinus, sat still in a chair across the room. The room was dark, cool in the summer's heat. I waited while my eyes grew accustomed to the lighting. Yes, it was Tigellinus, older, heavier but the same eye-catching kiss-of-the-gods looks which exuded power and privilege.

"It has been too long, Hylas."

"A long time indeed," I paused not quite knowing how to address him.

"Time has been kind to you," he said finally as he stood and beckoned me to a chair near the one he had occupied.

"Not as kind as it has been to you," I responded moving toward the offered chair.

He grinned and for a second I caught in it the Tigellinus of old. "That has always been my blessing from the Gods, and my curse. He stopped and grinned again. "But we've discussed that before, haven't we? The double edged sword of great beauty? Do you remember that conversation, what twenty years ago now? Has it been that long?" He poured wine and offered me a glass, very fine glass, the color of opals. "You do remember, don't you?"

"I do."

"Of course you do. Beauty was about to bring me down, just as it had brought you down through the mire as a boy. But it was about to set you free once again. Beauty takes us up and down at the whim of the Gods.

"And has beauty brought you up again?" I asked sipping on the cool mellow wine.

He grinned and nodded. "That and other things, Hylas. Still, I believe it was beauty that opened the door, way back when, even before Caligula and Agrippina. Before I knew you. I was aware of it at a young age and, like you, decided to make use of that to get what and where I wanted."

"I remember your pointing the way for me. It was good advice."

"It was your survival, Hylas. I was the one who taught you to stop thinking like the pretty little boy whore slave you were and to develop a direction that would lead to freedom. I gave you that, Numerius Meridius Pulcher. I put the gears of that brain of yours to work. I did that."

"You certainly put the idea in my head," I said carefully considering my options. It would be unwise to argue with him.

Caution was vital until I knew where this little speech was going. "You, made me aware, and yes, it changed my life."

He relaxed as quickly as he had tightened up a moment before. "Oh let's not bring all that up, Hylas. You helped me when I needed it most. I still think Caligula would have had my head that day had he found me."

I permitted myself the slightest of smiles. "Instead you were exiled."

He laughed. "Yes, and at the time it seemed the end of the world. But, as you see it wasn't, for here I am again. It took time, but here I am. This time I plan to stay." He smiled again and moved to a couch where he lay on his side propped up on an elegant elbow. "We have known each other for a long time, Hylas. We have been important to one another. I think I can say that there was a time when you favored me above all others, a time when..." He let the unfinished sentence hang in the air and smiling at me as he had when we were younger ran the tip of his long elegant finger around the rim of his glass. "Was I wrong, Hylas? You did, didn't you?"

I shook my head more to cover my surprise than in answer. "No, no..." I stumbled wildly for words that would cover where my brain was reeling. "You were not wrong. There was a time..." Why hadn't I seen it? It had been there all along, staring me in the face.

Tigellinus smiled broadly. "No, I won't force you to say it. It was after all a long time ago. But," he sat up and placing both hands on the firm matured thighs looked directly into my eyes, his own cold and hard with meaning. "I want you to remember and because you remember I want you to heed the advice that I am about to give you." He paused, no doubt for effect. "And, I suggest you take this advice as seriously as that I gave you all those years ago, Hylas. "Stay out of this Vestal thing. It will lead you nowhere you want to end up." He sat frozen, staring me down, making sure I received the message. "We have had too much in the past for me to want to see it end badly for you. Pausina has asked you to back down. She should have never involved you in the first place, but I wasn't here, and she had suddenly seen you that day; and...well, who knows the way women think?" He stood. "Now you're here and I'm the one telling you. Do not force the hand of an old admirer, Hylas. It could be a fatal error." He smiled and crossing to the chair put his hand under my chin and raised it toward him. "Amazing what a little magic with the cosmetic brush can accomplish, isn't it? Have you ever wanted to meet the emperor, Hylas? It could be arranged. Nero is fond of legends."

I knew better than to give him the answer that sprung to mind, but was uncertain how well I hid it in my eyes. I bit my tongue.

"Well," he smiled and dropping his hand moved away. "I guess not. As you wish, Hylas. But do please remember what I've said for the sake of our past, and your future." Turning his back he headed for a door that appeared to open onto a courtyard. "Someone will show you out, Hylas. It has been good to see you again despite the circumstances." He stopped at the door, turned and leaned against it with his arms crossed. His body caught the light from the courtyard and for a moment he looked once more much like the young man I had known all those years ago. "You're still beautiful, Hylas, older of course, but beautiful. Remember my invitation to meet the emperor. You might find him an interesting young man."

To my relief he didn't wait for a reply, simply turned and left the room. A moment later a guard entered and showed me the way out and to a side gate where I was once again free and alone on the street. I breathed in the air and started for Metella's on foot. It wasn't far and I had much to tell Aristo and the others, and even more to think about how to proceed or whether to proceed at all. I would be a fool not to take Tigellinus's warning seriously. It might be wiser for me to drop it all and go pick out fabrics for the new house, but I have never been one to blindly do what was wise. I needed time and time was in short supply. While I walked home the gears turned anew.

Chapter 18

The relief on Aristo's face when I walked into the house was both telling and endearing. I fully expected him to embrace me on the spot, but with Metella and others present he was in control, as usual. It would have been unseemly. Still, I knew. The rest looked likewise relieved. Even Burrus brightened. Obviously their thoughts about my heavy handed invitation had not been good ones and with good reason. Metella unhindered by protocol hugged me tightly. Young Quintus slapped my back while Apollo grinned and withdrew and Burrus called for wine.

"We were terrified, Numerius." Metella finally let go of my neck and looked up at me. "What was it all about? Who was it?"

"I need a bath," I said to Aristo who took off to see to it. "It was Tigellinus," I said to Metella. "I had heard he was back in the mix of things. I simply didn't realize how much so, or that he might be involved with this whole thing."

"How? How is Tigellinus involved?" Metella asked, worried anew.

"Tigellinus is not a man to be played with, Numerius," said Burrus. "People are summoned by Tigellinus and then disappear. What does that old goat have to do with this?"

I took the cup of wine from the tray that the slave entered with, offering me the goblet before refilling Burrus's with the pitcher. "Unless I'm horribly wrong, Tigellinus is the true father of our young Aronius. And my own eyes tell me that is the case. I knew that boy reminded me of someone. It bothered me since that first night I laid eyes on him. Today I saw that same young man, albeit older, in the face of Tigellinus. There is no mistake. He has to be the father. Which of course makes this whole affair rather more delicate."

"Maybe it is time to quit, Numerius." Metella said fingering her necklace, a habit when nervous. "You are in heady circles when Tigellinus is involved, dangerous circles."

"By Hades, lady, there's already a Chief Vestal and a pumped up Vestal involved," Burrus laughed, 'Can't get much headier than that. So what exactly did the old goat tell you?"

"Nothing much, certainly not that the boy is his son, just that he would very much appreciate it if I desisted."

Burrus chuckled. "I'll wager that wasn't the way he put it."

I smiled back at him. "More or less."

"I'm not sure that the solving of some puzzle that has absolutely nothing to do with me is sufficient reason for putting my family in danger, Numerius. Vestal or not, murder or not, my family comes first."

"He's not an idiot, Metella. He'll be careful whatever he does," countered Burrus.

It felt odd to have Burrus standing up for me. "I will be careful, Metella. You can count on that. I just need time to think, and that bath."

"Of course, you will," Metella said standing. "And don't dally too long. Dinner has already been pushed back once and the kitchen will be furious if I do it again."

"We mustn't upset the kitchen," said Burrus.

"Of course not. I'll be quick about it." I said heading off for my room and the warm bath I knew would be waiting for me. "I will join you shortly."

Aristo was waiting for me with the bath. The water was warm if not exactly hot. The best tub bath can't compare to our Roman baths, but they do the job. I would have liked the long drawn out process of the public baths but settled for the tub and expert hands of Aristo. In the new house we would have a proper bath right in the house, tepidarium, caldarium and frigidarium all right there for our convenience, complete with a small palaestra for exercise. I looked forward to it, that, on the condition that I managed to stay alive until then. I of course had to consider the safety of my sister and her family; nor was I ready to give up on my own life quite yet. Still, there was that part of me which was stubbornly urged on by Tigellinus's and Pausina's pressure on me to give up. I have never liked being told to keep my nose out of something. It rings all the wrong bells for me. If Tigellinus wanted me out of it, there was a very good chance that the boy was involved in the murder, but if that was all, then why would Pausina be waving me off? Unless of course Tigellinus had got to her as well. That didn't sound like the Pausina I knew. There had to be more to it. It was possible that she was just trying to protect me, but that, too, didn't sound like Pausina. As for Hesperia, Tigellinus's involvement explained a lot. He was undoubtedly the one paying for young Aronius's entertainment at the Golden Wing and if he had so much as dropped a hint to stay out of it she would have been foolish not to do so. That at least made me feel better about the way she had dealt with me. I couldn't truly fault her for that. The question was, could I get any more information out of her? No, Pausina was the one who knew more than she was telling and, I suspected, a lot more.

Aristo dried me off and helped me dress for dinner. I was late, but they had just finished the egg course so I certainly wouldn't go hungry. Squabs were next and I love squabs. We were barely into them when our attention was wrested away by pounding on the outside door, raised voices and Marcus Flavius bursting into the dining room. The boy was hot and flushed.

"They've stolen the baby!" he shouted at us from the doorway. "The baby's gone." He was near tears. I've just come back and the baby's gone, Laelia's baby. You have to get it back for me, Numerius. We have to find it and get it back. I must have her baby, Numerius. It's only right. They took her from me. I have a right to her baby. He should be mine. I have the right."

It was Metella who moved toward the boy first, followed by Quintus while the rest of us, Burrus, Lucia and I sat and gaped.

"Now, calm yourself, Marcus," she said, her motherly instinct taking over. "Calm yourself and tell us about it. It will be okay, just tell us all about it, Marcus." She took him into her arms. "Quintus get him some wine. He'll be okay. Let's just get him settled down a little. It will be all right, Marcus. Calm down now, so we can decided how to proceed. Shhh. Breathe. We'll figure this out." She took the wine from Quintus and gave it to the boy. "Here take a drink of this. You're tired and dusty and must be thirsty. Here..." She deftly maneuvered him to her place, sat him down and gave him the cup of wine. "Drink for a minute. Breathe deeply. We will wait."

The boy did as she advised. He was shaking, hot, sweaty and dusty no doubt from the road. He drank the wine taking the cup in both hands and guiding it to his lips.

"There now, that's better." Metella cooed as he drained the cup and set it on the table before him. "Now tell us what has happened."

The boy took a deep breath. "I had the baby. Chloe brought it to me. She didn't know what to do. She brought me the baby and then went back to get her things. I told her not to but she had to have her things. She never came back. I was going to take her with the baby to our place near Tibur. Father never goes there anymore. I thought I could keep them there until I decided what to do with them. How to convince father ... but she never came back. It was a boy, the prettiest baby boy I've ever seen, hers and Aronius's, a perfect baby, the perfect baby boy. He would have grown up like his father, I could see that in the little bundle's face. He was beautiful."

"Who knew about the baby?" I asked the boy quietly. "Who else knew? Aronius? Your father?"

The boy shook his head. "No one. I didn't tell father. I thought I would break it to him later, when the time was right. He was furious with Laelia. I thought I'd give him time to get used to the idea and then he would want the boy, his grandson, that he would accept him ... in time. And as for Aronius, I knew he didn't really want the baby. He was being nice about it, because I kept at him, but he really wasn't interested, I knew that. I knew that from the beginning. Things changed as soon as Laelia knew she was pregnant. He changed, backed off. I had to keep him to it. He would have left her completely otherwise. I could see that. He didn't want the baby. I had to do things to keep him at it, Numerius...things..." he looked from me to Metella, "things, I cannot tell you here. Horrible things, things that shame me, but I had to keep him seeing Laelia. I couldn't let her know how he felt. She loved him." His eyes had filled with tears. "She loved him and I loved him. But he loves no one, not her, not the baby, and certainly not me. He used us. He used us all."

"So, your father knew about it, knew about her being with child, knew about the baby? When did he find out? How long has he known? Since the beginning?"

Marcus shook his head. "No. Only since Pausina came to see him a few days before the baby was born; he had no idea before that. But he went into a rage. Mother was beside herself, shut herself up in her rooms, wouldn't eat, didn't come out for days. He knew that she had known... knew we both had been to see her countless times. He was furious with us all. He threatened to kill her himself, but I know he didn't, he couldn't kill his own daughter. I'm sure he's not the one who killed her, Numerius. He couldn't be, could he?" The boy broke down completely, tears runnin from his eyes, and once again Metella stepped in.

"Enough, enough now, Marcus. Of course he couldn't have, no father could," she lied. "You need a bath. Numerius, take Marcus to your rooms and have Aristo arrange a bath for him. The two of you can talk in there. He doesn't need an audience. Take him and be careful with him; he needs to rest, Numerius. Quintus, Lucia, go about your business. Burrus you certainly have something to do. It's time to do it. Let the boy have some peace and privacy. Take him, Numerius."

I did as I was instructed. I took the sobbing boy to my rooms where Aristo arranged for a bath and we put the boy into the steaming water and let him soak.

For several minutes we sat in silence. I watched the tears stream down the boy's face. "He didn't love her, Numerius," he said finally. "Not really. It was all a game for him. Just like me, I was...a game for him too...and...he made me do terrible things in order to agree to keep seeing her... Degrading, disgusting things, first with him and then with others while he watched...Hateful, mean things.

He used me, made money off of me...and laughed about it. Some horrible..."

"There, now," I interrupted. "That's enough, my boy. Don't forget who you're talking to. I know how it is to be used. I understand. I understand completely. It is survivable. You go on. They can only shame you if you allow them. You had a reason. You needn't be ashamed anymore. You were doing it to protect Laelia. That was honorable regardless of what others might think. Put it behind you now."

My heart ached for the boy. It was true enough what I had told him. I knew how it was to be humiliated and used by those who wanted to shame one, unspeakable desires of unspeakable men whose only thrills came from forcing someone else to wallow in the mire seemingly lower than they themselves. I had known such men and hated them from my very core.

By the time I had gotten the boy bathed, settled and bedded down for the night, my head was already redirected toward piecing together the next move. There were several questions I wanted answered besides finding the baby, and Pausina figured in more than one of them. It struck me as strange that all the while knowing about Laelia she had chosen to go to the girl's father only just before the birth. Why had she done such a thing? What had she suspected? I also wanted to know just how she and Tigellinus figured together in this. He himself had let me know about that connection during our meeting by alluding to her sending for me because he was out of town. I wanted to know just how involved the two of them were. There was no way to avoid another trip to see Pausina and she would not be happy about it.

But there was nothing to be done so late in the evening, and I was starving as our dinner had been interrupted, so I instructed Aristo to set up a late night supper for the two of us in the garden with whatever leftovers he could scavenge from the kitchen. He looked at the naked young man asleep on my bed and raised an eyebrow. I reassured him with a shake of my head and he pattered off to the kitchen. Just like him to jump immediately to the thought that even under such circumstances I might have found the time and inclination. Well, I suppose over the years I have given him reason for concern. It was after our quiet dinner while I lay in an unfamiliar bed in a room other than my own that I began to put the pieces together. The night passed slowly my sleep disturbed by the churning of my mind and how next to proceed. By the time dawn began to spill through the shuttered window I was ready to rise and get on with it.

Chapter 19

I was nearly dressed for my visit to Pausina when a slave entered with a message that a rather unsavory hulk of a man waited for me at the door. Andronicus had not liked the looks of him at all and refused him entry until I personally took a look at the man. With my recent run in with the men of Tigellinus, I decided it was a good idea to check him out.

It was Vorax, my bully-boy from the house of Flavius. On a mission but pleased to be seeing me again.

"You must come with me, sir. The Mistress wants you to come at once. A terrible thing has happened. Marcus Flavius is dead,I will say that much. Suicide it looks to me. The young master has not returned yet either She says you must come at once. She is beside herself over it and worried sick about what may have happened to the young one."

"Wait for me here," I said. "I am nearly ready and as for the boy, he is here already. It will take a moment to get him up and dressed" For the briefest of moments the man's face flashed a look of amusement. I stopped ready to deny it, but decided it wasn't the time and turned to go and wake Marcus. "Just wait here." I headed for my rooms and the unpleasant task of breaking the news to Marcus. I hate getting stuck with the dirty jobs. Still, it had fallen to my lot and I would do it.

It did not take us long to be on our way.

The house of the Flavii was in mourning. Slaves gathered in quiet groups always fearful in such circumstances lest one of their number be blamed for the death and the ensuing punishment that could possibly come down on all of them.   Sulpicia, the widow and mother of Marcus was an imposing woman and the parent from whom Marcus and Laelia obviously got their looks. Greatly relieved to see her son with us, she embraced him unconcerned for the display of unRoman-like emotion. I was pleased to see that young Marcus responded in kind. I thought I could detect even Aristo softening a little toward the boy. Perhaps there was more there than we had first thought. I let the family reunion play out briefly before turning to the business at hand.

In his study, Marcus Flavius the elder lay carefully across the couch I had so recently been seated on. The pools of dark dried blood from his slashed wrists nearly converged onto one another beneath the couch.

"He left two messages," Sulpicia said, "the one for me telling me to send for you, and this one for you." She stepped to his desk and retrieved the still sealed note addressed to me which, once handed to me, I opened.

Numerius Meridius Pulcher.

Salve:

What I have done I have done out of honor for our family. My daughter is dead and disgraced and I have seen to it that the boy is likewise. I may be old   and brittle but I am not incapable of murder with the proper assistance, despite what Pausina may think. That detestable boy did not deny being the father of my daughter's child. In fact he seemed to find it rather amusing.

He was easily lured here by pretense of a meeting with my son. In short the young man proved to be all I fear for the future of Rome. I do not regret having eliminated even just this one viper from Rome. It seems we are headed once again for the excesses and vileness of the reign of that most hated of emperors, Caligula. I no longer wish to see it. I neither want to see my daughter disgraced in the eyes of Rome, nor do I want to partake in the cover up of such sacrilege. I have done want I felt necessary. I have led a good and honorable life after a somewhat depraved youth as you were witness to. My apologies to you for not giving you the same benefit of doubt when I saw you enter my house. It is not easy for a reformed man to face his unsavory and distant past so unexpectedly. Whether or not I would approve of the person you have become, I will never know. I do, however ask you sincerely to do what you can to protect my family.

Vale;

Marcus Flavius Sulla

I read the above and felt rather sorry for the old fool who had written it. He had been a throw back to an earlier time, a time when Rome and her leaders were about honor. Having sown his wild oats in his youth, he had grasped firmly the   values of the old and forgotten Republic. His honor was saved, but at what cost? I handed the wax tablet to Marcus with instructions that he destroy it.   No good would come from it getting outside of myself, his wife and his son. As for me,I needed to see Pausina before the news of Aronius's death got around. The letter had put the final pieces together for me, now all I needed was confirmation and a good bluff.

I left the wife with her son and the dead but honorable Flavius.

Chapter 20

Pausina did not want to see me. She kept me waiting at the side entrance to the House of the Vestals until I threatened to return in my easily recognizable litter and wait for her convenience at front the front gate so that the entire forum would be witness to my visit. She received me in a small writing room.

"I do not like being threatened, Numerius. It is unwise for you to do so. You should know that of me."

I bowed slightly.   "I have no intention to threaten you, Pausina. Only to bring you the facts as you originally instructed me to."

"The facts? I am no longer interested in the facts."

"Be that as it may, Pausina, I am. I have never been able to walk away from an unsolved puzzle and I have had to figure this one out. I always have to find the answers, as you should know of me."

"I could bring you down, Hylas. I could do it here and now."

"From where exactly? I haven't so far to fall as I am not in such a lofty position as you."

She shifted in her chair, uncomfortable with my insinuation. "What is it that you think you know? You might as well tell it to me and be done with it. I don't like playing games."

"Marcus Flavius Sulla has committed suicide."

She paused and shrugged but her eyes belied her interest. "Not a great loss for Rome and considering his daughter's sacrilege not to be totally unexpected. So why bring me this news? You must have more than that?"

"And I do.   Actually it was his message to me that finally slipped all the pieces into place. I'm not sure he saw it clearly, but I surely did. Just as I knew I had to come and tell you the whole story."

She drew herself up in her chair her voice hard flat, demeaning. "And what makes you think I don't know the whole story?"

"Oh, you know most of story. That is a given, but only most, Pausina. I suspected you were unaware of it all..suspected until you received me just a few minutes ago and then I was quite sure." I paused, knowing the necessity and the effect it would have on my one time friend. "You don't know the reason Flavius killed himself."

"And, I suppose you feel the need to tell me. Oh, I could not care less why that old fool did anything."

"Young Quintus is dead." I dropped the bowl of boiling oil and watched for the splatter. It came instantly. Pausina flinched and paled beneath the artfully applied cosmetics, her hands started for and were pulled back from her throat. She trembled but said nothing but her eyes might have slashed me to tiny pieces. I decided to go on. "So it's true. Anyone who knew Tigellinus all those years ago as well as we did would instantly be able to spot Quintus Aronius as his son. The rest was put to me with Flavius's letter. Just a memory of an old rumor. Knowing Tigellinus as I do, as I did, I should have already thought of it, but time shadows things. I had put it out of my mind. I wasn't the only thing Tigellinus had to have. Like everything denied him - an emperor's sister, Rome's most notorious whore, and you Rome's loveliest Vestal...he had to have them all. I should have realized sooner. And now you have confirmed it, Pausina. Aronius is your son by Tigellinus."

Pausina stiffened regally, but her eyes filled with tears. "I confirm nothing, Hylas. Nothing at all."

"Well, regardless of your willing confirmation or not, I have come to strike a bargain."

"You dare bargain with me?"

"It is all written down, Pausina. And will be taken to the proper authorities if need be." I bluffed my threat and went forward. It was all written down and it would be taken to the proper authorities but in Rome one could never be sure what direction things would take then. "How you and Tigellinus conceived a child. How you supported that grown child's affair with Laelia and how you, Pausina, planned to take their child in replacement of the child taken from you."

"Why by the Gods would I do such a thing, it would be putting my child at risk, if what you say is true. Doesn't sound too convincing to me. I don't think anyone would believe this written report even if you did disappear. "

I took a breath and readied to put forward my final ploy, hoping it would float. "No, perhaps not right now...but it would bring the rumors back up to mind. And then next year when you retired from your duties here and suddenly reports of a baby taken into your household began to leak out...well, if you managed to escape full exposure and retaliation, the rumors would follow you and the child for the rest of your lives."

"So where is the bargain in all this and I still admit to nothing."

"The bargain is this.   For the two murders and a kidnapping..."

"What, how dare you." She nearly flew out of her chair toward me.

"Well, you have the child, I have no doubts about that. The murders...well, it was that Greek physician of yours was it not? Laelia and Chloe. Chloe once you'd found out what she'd done with the baby. Laelia either because she resisted your plan or simply to remove the eventual claim she might lay to child."

"I hate you, Numerius Meridius Pulcher. You have no idea how much I hate you. I wish Caligula had killed you when he had the chance.   Everyone knew you were marked to die before he was assassinated and that old fool Claudius had a soft spot for you and let you off." She laughed harshly, then continued in her most vitriolic voice. "And we all thought the old bugger didn't have the itch for the pretty boys, but I guess you proved us all wrong. You dare approach me for having broken my vow with one man when you have slept with all the scum of Rome since old Tiberius? You make me sick to my stomach." She returned to her chair relieved by her outburst. "So tell me about this bargain, little man; if I can use such a term with you. You are no man, as we both know. So give, Hylas. Give me your bargain."

I struggled not to lash back, but I had won. Her spew of hate showed me that. I needed to move on not strike back in kind. I bit my tongue and moved on to my terms.

"The child is to be delivered to his other grandmother. It is only fitting as you have taken her child. I, on the other hand, will tell no one, not even the family, not even Tigellinus, exactly what I have found out. I will have simply located the child."

"And the questions that follow?" Pausina looked at me through deadened eyes. She'd known defeat before. This was not her first taste.

"Let me handle that. I can assure you the whole affair ends there."

She looked at me silently for a moment before speaking. Despite her guilt it was not pleasant for me to wound an old one time friend such. "Tigellinus was right. It was a mistake to contact you. I could have found the baby on my own."

"So he told me and so you did."

"You saw Tigellinus?"

"Not by choice. Let us say he saw me."

She sighed and shook her head. "I never saw his attraction. He has always had a soft spot for you. I suggested he get rid of you. It would have been so much easier."

"Lucky for me he didn't"

"Yes, lucky for you. What shall I tell him now?"

"I'll let you handle him, Pausina since you have a long history of it."

"Get out, Hylas. And stay well away from me in the future. I will not forget this. Watch for me to come at you when you least expect it. Sulpicia will have her grandson, the grandson that should be mine, is mine, but be warned... you should tread carefully in Rome. Go back to Pompeii where all retired whores belong."

That lash had lost its sting. "As you wish," I said bowing. "By this evening; or, I go where I need to go."

She didn't look up, she sat slumped in her chair, an old defeated woman and for a moment I felt sorry for her, before I realized that I was really feeling sorry for a young girl I had known long ago and not the woman she had become. "Get out." She whispered after several moments. "Get out. We're done, Numerius."

Epilogue

I had been relieved to leave Pausina and the House of the Vestals.   My return to the house on Palatine was leisurely and thoughtful. Later I would dress and wait for the news of the arrival of a baby.   The child could easily be passed off as one of young Marcus's youthful misadventures.   It would work, and I couldn't resist hinting at the news to Metella without promising in case something went amiss. It didn't and I was even more relieved when a messenger arrived to fetch me to their home on the Quirinal. The child had indeed been delivered that very night to the House of the Flavii as promised. I was able to watch as Sulpicia and young Marcus were lifted from the blackness of their mourning by the tiny bundle of life. Time would soon soothe their losses with the blessing of the little one the Fates have given in return, a child that would carry the name Numerius in addition to the prescribed family names. It was a gracious and sentimental thing to do, but Sulpicia and Marcus were sincerely both. I only hoped that the boy would never fully recognize for whom he had been named. Still it pleased me to think about Pausina's reaction. She would find out. There would be no way to keep her from the knowledge and the fact that it would niggle at her for the rest of her days pleased me much more than it should have.

As for me and Aristo, we set about seeing to the finishing of the new house in Rome and within the fortnight moved in with our staff which now had grown to include Apollo and, through the ministrations of Aristo and a very kind Quintus Aronius, Phillipia, her husband and the twins. For someone who started out a slave and basically disapproves of the practice, I seem to be always acquiring more of them wherever I go.

There were times when I worried about Pausina and what revenge she might bring down on us all. I knew to avoid her and having no idea how much she had told Tigellinus worried some about him as well; but, the spring slipped by into the summer and then on into the fall. Life as the gods ordained, was taken up with other things.

The End